MCKINZEY'S REVENGE

MICHAEL LEE

Cover concept: Michael Lee
Cover artist: Jaycee DeLorenzo, Sweet 'N Spicy Designs.
She is a master at her craft.

Chief Editor: Kate Richards,
Content and line editor: Laura Garland. Nanette Sipe.
Special contributing editor: Ward Beckham

Publishing Coordinator – Sharon Kizziah-Holmes

Paperback-Press
an imprint of A & S Publishing
Paperback Press, LLC
Springfield, Missouri

ISBN -13: 978-1-960499-78-3

DEDICATION

To my good friend and buddy, Robert Giel. He never lost faith in me. See you at the next Rendezvous. You're buying!

Acknowledgments

"OUT OF CHAOS COMES CLARITY"

Behind every author and completed project book, lies a bevy of unheralded names and faces:

Clarissa Willis. Thank you for your trust and honesty, guidance and patience.

The Critique Me Friday 6: Straw Boss Skiz (Sharon Kizziah-Holmes), Thriller Beast (J. C. Fields), Reigning Regency Queen (Conetta Taylor), Mystery Romancer (Shirley King McCann), (Romance Icon) Lori Copeland. I consider y'all, as contributing editors. Thank you. You hold a special place in my heart...My Best to you always...Pick-a-Toe Joe.

Others have contributed to this project in many ways. Encouragement is always appreciated from them.

CLASS OF 1968, WARREN CENTRAL HIGH SCHOOL, INDIANAPOLIS, INDIANA! You, all have been a blessing. Brenda Williams Meredith, my true friend. Adam Lee, Abigail Lee, my children. Staff at Bass Pro in Springfield, Missouri, they have been friends and readers.

*My good friend, Renetta Reaves introduced me, to her author cousin, Heather Burch. Renetta knew I was a writer and she wanted to introduce us. Heather lived in Kansas City and we (?) never met, as she passed soon thereafter. She was young and vibrant in her pictures and stories Renetta related to me. A brilliant loss... I was welcomed into a critique group as a member had moved away. Unbeknownst to me, this was Heathers seat I occupied. In some way, I knew Heather before I found my group. We are all connected by stardust. Much love to you, Heather Burch. In the Critique group, Heather was Women's Woman.

*Special thanks to Darrel Rader and John Hart of the NRA Sporting Arms Museum at Bass Pro in Springfield, Missouri. This is a wonderful museum. Joe Wood was our tour guide and wonderful teller of tales for me and my friend, Bob Giel. They were a font of knowledge on gun history and weaponry.

NOTE FROM THE AUTHOR

I have had a long fascination with the early civilizations of this country. The more I learn, the more I am impressed that the native cultures developed architecture, trade, food resources in parallel to those European and Asian counterparts. It is a shock to most when they realize the majority of the food used by the planet were developed by Native Americans. As the Europeans sought land in the new country, that clash of cultures built the foundation of what "The American Spirit" became.

My stories are a mix of history and myth, hero and villain. The good didn't always win. The villain wasn't completely evil. The good guy had a bit of villain within himself as well. They are stories of perseverance, luck and sometimes, just plan damn stubbornness.

My wish is to share that independence, the raw, tough sinuousness of the men and women, both native and pioneer that manifested as the "Spirit of America" with my reader.

Chapter 1

April 1853 Salem, Oregon

Everything was as he'd dreamed it. Jonny McKinzey followed the Willamette River south, riding toward Salem, Oregon, looking for his father's ranch and mill. The hills awash in spring's green, bright and verdant, burst with innocent expectation and the vitality of new life. Willamette Falls blew a throaty roar as he passed. Farther down the river, steamers pulled barges filled with lumber and passengers, who waved to him as they churned upstream to new destinations.

His father's letter was in his pocket, giving him directions to their new ranch and instructing him to finish up his schooling, sell their old ranch, and join him and his adopted brother, Shepherd, in Oregon. After seven hard months on the trail, he was yearned to be reunited with his family. The money from the sale of their Indiana ranch would be the key to their future in Oregon.

Jon saluted the river's call and began whistling a tune he had learned on the steamboat, about a sailor having a girl in every port. Gusty air blew down from the mountains, urging him toward his new home.

Almost giddy with expectation, Jonny was a rich young

man with his entire life spread out in front of him. "Get up there, you old nag."

Reaching down, he stroked his horse's neck. "Sorry, girl," he soothed her. "I just want to see my new home."

He planned to share that life with his father, and his adopted brother, Shepherd, but he had to get to the ranch first. Memories flooded over him of conversations they had before his father and brother left.

A flour mill on the river was Shep's idea. "People has got to have bread. There's all that river going to waste. Let's plan to use it."

So, they took the hard-to-get hardware and several millstones with them when they left.

"Lots of forests as well, boys. Lots of opportunity. Though none of us can make any guarantees, I think we're on the right track." Daddy John, or Mac as he was called, talked as they sat around the fire, planning their trip. "Probably lots of sawmills. We will do better with a grindin' mill. After"—he held a finger up—"we finish the house." He clapped Shepherd on the back and winked at young Jon. "You finish your schoolin', get all the book learnin' you can. Sell the stock a little at a time at top price. You're savvy enough to be a good horse trader. Then sell the ranch and get out there as fast as you can. Maybe you can get a job with some outfit in Independence. You won't have much but your clothes and them guns I give you."

He paused and put his favorite meerschaum pipe back in his mouth. "I know I don't have to say this, Jon, but for your own safety, never mention the money you carry to nobody. Just a father's concern. I trust you. You know that. It's the other scallywags, I don't trust. Shep and me can finish the house. But..." He held everyone's attention with a bright grin. "Shep and me is gonna have some of the rankest hosses for you to break when you get there. Mark my word!" He slapped his knee and pointed at young Jonny.

Both he and Shepherd chuckled at Jonny's red face. They knew he could ride with the best of them.

"You do that, you two. I'll ride every one of them. I been riding and breaking horses since I was ten. I can ride anything that jumps, humps, and sneezes. Can't wait to get there."

"McKinzey's will be known for their horses again. That'll make me feel just fine, it will." Mac sat back in his chair, smoking his pipe. "Yes, sir, that will make me feel just fine."

A group of buildings loomed up on Jonny's right. That would be the Indian Training School and Methodist mission his father said to look for. The family ranch should be just another five miles or so on the other side of a small group of sloping hills, just up from the river.

Jonny Mac rode on, eager to get there. He slapped his leg in excitement. "Wait till they see me. I can't wait to see them." His heart raced with joy and anticipation at the thought of being home at last. "I can't wait to see Shep."

They had grown up together north of Indianapolis, Indiana. Jonny was a strapping boy of six feet tall, but Shep towered over him by another four inches. A bone of friendly contention all of their youth.

The miles went by as if in a dream, memories of his boyhood came to him. The McKinzey ranch was a horse ranch, breaking and training horses of any breed or need. Shep and he spent their young, more limber days breaking and training the rough stock that came in. Early on, gentling horses for ladies riding and for carriages had been their specialty. Later, as Indianapolis grew, the demand for teamster stock and mules to pull wagons west became their main source of business. The call west was a magnet pulling at Mac McKinzey's heart.

The long lines of wagons moving west had caught John Mac's attention. It had been a long time since he had felt a challenge to his manhood and mind. It roused his spirit. His excitement built. Traffic moving west occupied his mind. Going west developed into a lust that had infected him, and he determined to go.

"If your mother was here, I'd probably stay in Indianapolis, but that Greeley man, telling me to go west, has got in my blood, I tell you. There are no guarantees in life. I've come to understand that, since my Martha was taken." He began making immediate plans to go. Two years ago, he did.

Shep had decided to go with him, and both would build a home expecting Johnny after he finished his school. "I know you want to go with us, little brother, but one of us has got to get an education. Because of my skin, they won't let me, but you? You gots to do it for both of us."

It had been a challenging adventure coming to Oregon. Now it was at the finish.

He slapped the reins over the horse's back. "I want to see the look on Shep and Pa's faces." He stood in the stirrups trying to see ahead. The ranch should be just below the top of the next rise they were climbing.

"Here it comes now, home and family, next stop." He whistled aloud to pick up the pace, snapping the reins over his horse's rump, moving her almost to a run. "Finally." He shouted the word then it caught in his throat. He sat down with a hard thump. His gut twisted into knots of pure disbelief.

There was nothing. Nothing was where he had pictured his ranch in his mind. The scene was all wrong. He swallowed hard and looked around. Perhaps he had taken a wrong turn.

Chapter 2

1841 Indianapolis, Indiana
McKinzey ranch

"Whoa up there, my baby!" John "Mac" McKinzey flicked his whip over the back of the horse he had on a long lead rope in a circular pen. "Up ya go, my baby, that's it." He stopped. Gooseflesh rippled up his spine. He turned toward the sound. Someone was crying for help.

A figure was running wildly through the pasture, screaming its heart out. "Help. Help. They hung my ma and pa! They burned us up."

John Mac looked up, seeing black sooty smoke, and white clouds of billowing smoke rose behind the running figure. He bolted for the barn.

"What is it, Pa?" Jonny stood looking at the figure running toward them, shading his eyes with his hand. "Who is it?"

"I suspect it is that young Negra boy, whose family lives down the road. I think his name is Shepherd. Stay here. Call your ma. I'm going down there."

John swung up barebacked on the closest horse, kicking with his heels, anrode out to the little figure, gesturing for him to go to the house. Climbing down off the horse, he took off his shirt and wrapped it around the boy, whom he discovered running naked in the field. He remounted, pointing and telling the boy to run to the house.

As Mac rode up to the house, he saw flames licking the sky, blistering grass and tree leaves in every direction. Two hooded bodies hung from a huge Sycamore's limb, swinging as the heat gusts were fanned by the western breezes. Smoke tendrils rose from the man and woman's clothes. John cut them down with his knife. After sliding off his horse, he dragged the bodies out of the waves of heat. The shrouded hoods did little to hide who they were.

A young Creole couple who had come up out of the South, scratching out a living on the forty acres. The closest place down the hill to the McKinzey ranch.

John peeled the hood off the head of the man, instantly regretting his action. The skin was blistered and shredding off the face. John's stomach revolted, and he lost his breakfast in the dust.

"I can't let the kid see them this way." He replaced the hood loosely.

Fiery plumes raced skyward as the house's roof caved in. John shielded his eyes and pulled the bodies back out of the heat farther than before. Ash and tiny embers stung his skin and face.

The barn still stood. John found a pick and shovel. Grim determination sculpted his face as he dug. "What damn shameless animals, who call themselves God fearing men, could have done this?" he shouted to soothe his pent-up anger. "These were decent folk. They worked hard. They never did anything to man or beast. God bless them."

John cursed and sang old hymns from memory, holding back the tears and desperate grief that gripped his heart. "We will gather at the river. The beautiful, beautiful riiivver."

Digging like a mad man, he burned the mounting

emotion wracking his soul. He couldn't bear to see the fiery burned flesh again, so he left the hoods on as he dragged them into the comfort of the cool earth and tossed the sod back over them.

"Dust to dust, they say. Matt and Josey Bienville, I don't know who did this, but they will pay. Don't you worry none. I'll take charge of Shepherd. He's a good kid. I'll take him as one of my own. I know him a little, and I won't let nothing happen to him. I give you my word and hand on that." He raised his right hand, looked up to God, and bowed his head.

The walls of the house fell in on themselves, sending another fiery blast across the yard, blowing off John's hat and blinding his eyes.

"I didn't want Shepherd to see his ma and pa like that. I want him to remember you, Matt, as a strong tall man and his ma, pretty, like she was." John walked around the graves, kicking at clods and smoothing the top of the graves as he spoke. "You was good people. No one deserves this." He took off his hat then closed his eyes, raising his voice so it could be heard over the fire.

"Welcome these folk into their new home in heaven, Father. I can vouch for them. They was fine folks, always took care of their place and stock and each other. Matt, a fine man with horses, and Josey kept a clean house and set a good table. They was good neighbors to me and Martha and our boy, Jonny. Bless these good folk, Lord. Seat them at your table and forgive them of whatever sin they may have done. In his Holy name. Amen. I know you don't make no guarantees, Lord, but I gotta let Matt and Josey know I will find whoever did this. I have my suspicions, but they will show themselves, sooner or later."

John looked up the hill toward his ranch house. His heart lurched. He was going to have to tell Shepherd in some way that wouldn't scar the child for life. "God, give me the right words to say, 'cause I don't know them." He bowed his head.

CHAPTER 3

"**N**o. This is the right place." He read his father's letter again. "The river is there. Kalapuya rock is on my right." The rock with a strong native warrior profile was solidly in place, exactly where his pop had said it would be.

Jonny rubbed his eyes and stood up in the stirrups. The burned entrance sign had fallen. He rode over to it. McK, it started, but the rest was too charred to read. "This is where I should be. Right here."

Slowly, his brain tried piecing it all together. Charred beams from the house and barn lay scattered about, poking through the tall grasses shimmering from the wind, blown in from the west, as if they were sea grasses tossed by a current.

In the weeds along the riverbank, he could make out the waterwheel from the mill lying despondently on its side—dry, useless. Vines twisted around, growing through the blackened spokes, leaving only verdant mystery, full of questions and no answers.

In a state of shock, he rode down the hill to where this ranch once stood. A happy place?

As if in a dream, he climbed down from his horse, desperately searching for anything he could identify. Char and the smell of old smoke his throat and lips with a bitterness he could taste, as he walked about kicking at lumps of debris. Near the chimney, a bit of twisted, rusted metal caught his foot and he nearly fell. He rubbed the ash away on what remained of his father's shotgun, barely able to make out Purdy Manufacturing on the corroded brass.

Disbelief gave way to desperation. Uttering a cry of soul-sucking despair, he ran back to his horse, afraid the sight of the ruin and wreckage would undo his mind. He couldn't look any longer. Leaning against his saddle, Jonny stared at the ground beneath his feet, unable to raise his eyes to the haunting specter about him.

Reality overwhelmed. Burying his face in his arms, he cried deep anguished sobs, enveloped in wave after wave of disbelieving grief. He dried his eyes on his sleeve then looked at the scene again, trying to comprehend and rationalize it. The knots came again. Then, the truth dawned on him. The phrase his father had repeated many times echoed into his head, reverberating over and over, stopping him cold with dreaded reality.

There are no guarantees.

"There are no guarantees!" He'd repeated them often during his journey to Oregon each time tragedy struck, trying to make sense of what was happening. Now, he understood. He felt the meaning to the very depth of his core. It twisted his heart with an unrelenting grip.

A silhouette of a rounded white stone, out of place amongst the greenery, caught his eye over the side of the saddle. Tucked into the hedges and pink flowering rose bushes and redbud trees was a grave with a fresh clean marker. Sunshine blinded him, and he squinted, trying to focus.

Hesitating at first, he made his way toward it, forcing each step. He wished he could turn and hide from what he knew must be written on the slab. His faltering steps turned into a trot then into a full run. He had to know. He must know.

He already knew, because his gut told him it was true, but he had to see what the words said for himself.

Johnathon "Mac" David McKinzey, Beloved father. Beloved friend. Taken from us in the year 1852 by men unknown.

Grief swept over him, crashing him afresh against the unyielding rocks of despair and helplessness. "No. Oh my God, no! Pa. I've lost you?" His legs buckled, and he fell to his knees.

Memories of their life together came flooding back. The three of them raising horses. The fights. The hard work. Not so hard now. The long journey they had taken at different times on the Oregon trail after so many years apart, to bring them to this moment, rekindled the lost bond between father and sons.

The home they had lived in together, he and Pa and Shepherd, brought them a camaraderie only family could experience. They had laughed and drank beer, sweated in the warm sunshine, and forged a brotherhood only experienced by men who create with their own hands. It had been a dream. A remembered dream that washed over him as grief gripped his heart. His lonely journey among strangers and the few friends he'd made as he crossed the great barriers of plains, mountains, and evil men came to this heartbreak? He was finally home with loved ones? His thoughts hit a brick wall, and hope and joy slipped away.

"I should have been here. I could have helped. This should not have happened. I can't bear to lose you!" Crumpled by his father's grave, Jonny gave in to a cresting tide of unrequited guilt and grief, until all thought of time and place had vanished. He beat the ground. He kicked. He fought it, until he succumbed to the inevitable.

"Where's Shepherd?" There was no other grave. "Where's my brother?"

It was dark when he came to his senses. Night winds

ruffled his hair, cooled his face, and dried his eyes. His muscles ached, and he rolled onto his back, looking up at the starry night sky. His fists clenched handfuls of sodded earth.

After shaking the dirt from his hands, he rubbed them on his pants as he stood, realizing his mouth was filled with dirt and sod as well.

"I don't think I can swallow." The words stuck in his throat. Stumbling to the well, he spit the dirt from his mouth then drank deeply from the pail. He dumped the rest of it over his head. "The horse. I've forgotten about the horse."

Numb, stiff fingers unsaddled the standing animal. Jonny let the saddle drop and left it there, allowing the horse roam. He didn't care at this point. Shivering in his damp clothes, he leaned against a tree, staring into the oblivion before him. For something? No, there was nothing. Only unexplained anguish.

Digging into the saddlebags, he found a few blankets then returned to the grave. He lay, empty and exhausted, staring at the millions of cascading stars swirling above the place where John "Mac" McKinzey rested. Caught up in the vastness of the spectacle overhead, he talked to his pa as if he were sitting next to him.

"What happened here, Pa? Where's Shepherd? Where is he? What about the horses you planned to have? I don't understand how there's nothing left." He pondered the questions racing through his mind. Slowly, the pieces of the puzzled coalesced. *This was no accident! Somebody was responsible for this massacre. They had been deliberately attacked. Where was Shepherd?*

He glanced around then back to his father. "I'm sorry, Pa. We always worked better as a team. The three McKinzeys. Who could have done this to us? I blame myself. I could have done something. I'll find them, Pa. I'll find whoever did this. The cowardly bastards. I'll make them pay. I swear I'll find them and kill them all." Resolution built inside him, forging into an ironclad oath to his father.

He spoke as if the father he loved lay next to him, intently listening to his every word, sharing the plans they had dreamed of before they left Indiana. "I want to make this ranch the best in the Willamette valley, just like you intended to do, Pa." He stopped, hearing in his mind what his father would say, nodding in agreement. As the night deepened, Jonny told him of his journey on the trail and what he had done and seen.

Looking up at the sky, he spoke in a hushed voice. "I wish you would be here to see your grandbabes growing up on the ranch. We'll build again, Shepherd and me. We'll have a family I expect. You'd be their grandpa, ya know."

He listened to Mac's reply, smiling at the words. On into the night, he talked with his father until, totally spent and drained, he whispered one last promise as he fell asleep, sleeping this last sleep, next to his father.

"I'll find them, Pa. I'll kill them all."

CHAPTER 4

L yle Newton stepped outside Becky Palmer's café. He yawned before leaning against the wall next to the window, chewing on a toothpick while relishing the aftermath of one of Becky's good breakfasts. The weather had turned cold. *I better get my coat. It's going to rain soon.*

He stepped into the street, looking both ways so mud wouldn't get on his new pants. Waving to everyone who waved to him, Lyle made his way avoiding deep holes and sloppy ground, waving to everyone who caught his attention. While stomping his boots off on the sidewalk, Lyle looked up to see a bareback rider charging up to the hitching rail, scattering sodden clods and horse apples up on the sidewalk and onto his boots.

"Sheriff, could I have a word?" Jon said indifferently, sliding off his horse onto the boardwalk. Passing the town's sheriff, he marched up the sidewalk toward the office.

"Any time, young fella," said Lyle. "Passin' through? I haven't seen you around here." He moved forward, offering to shake hands. "Lyle Newton. You seem in a hurry. Is there a problem?" Lyle studied the young man's face. "What's your name, son? Maybe, I can help."

"McKinzey. Jonny McKinzey. My family had a ranch

here. I found it yesterday. It is all burned up! My pa is dead and buried!"

"You're Jonny McKinzey? By God, I've been hoping you would get here. You know the worst of it if you've been out there. Your father and brother are friends of mine. Sorry about your pa. Nothin' any of us could do. We didn't find them till three days after it happened."

"You know? Where's Shepherd? Where's my brother? What the hell happened out there?"

"Shepherd's over in the mission. They have a doctor and beds. They act as our hospital until we get one built. Let's go. I'll ride with you."

"Soo? Who did this, and are they in jail, Sheriff Newton?" Jon McKinzey sat barebacked as though he had been born to horses.

Lyle's appreciation went up.

"Shepherd was the only witness. He's been shot, twice. One in the leg and one that grazed his temple. The smoke and fire injured his lungs. He had a difficult time breathing. He swears he's going after the gang, but he can't do anything for a while. Doc took his boots and pants."

"That so," said Jon. "Tell me about this gang you mentioned. Where are they? Who was the leader? Why are they still on the loose?" When the mission came into view, Jonny sped on ahead.

Lyle rushed to catch up. "The questions you asked are best answered by Shepherd. He will be happy to see you. He has asked about you every day." When they reached the mission, Lyle climbed down then opened the door for Jon. "He's down that hall, last door on your right. C'mon, I'll show you."

A nurse stepped out into the hall from the room Sheriff Newton indicated. "Hi ya, Sister Donna. How's the patient?" He motioned for Jon to go through the door as he opened it. "Shep, got somebody here for you."

Shep McKinzey wore a bandage around his head. His

chest and back were wrapped in white linen. Mild bloodstains marked the deepest wounds. His right leg was strapped between two boards, and his right foot was bandaged as all the rest.

"Jonny! It is good to see you, finally." His face beamed.

"I've been to the ranch, Shep. I just come from there. I saw Pa's grave. Spent the night there, lying next to his side." He just stood, staring at his brother. "Sorry, Shepherd, it is a sad time. I am glad to see you are alive." He bent over to shake his hands, but he couldn't find a hand that wasn't in bandages. "Tell me what happened, Shepherd. Who killed Pa, crippled you, and burned us out?"

Shepherd returned Jon's remark, with a knowing look on his face. "You remember Whitey Nolan?"

"Whitey Nolan? You mean from Indiana? Them Nolans?"

"Same ones. They found us, Jonny. Out of nowhere one night, they started shooting up the house. Pa and I held them off for a while, before they fired the house. We ran to the barn and stable. Pa went to the corral to let the stock out before they burned up, when Whitey rode up and shot him in the back. Shot him all six shots of his gun. Then he ran the horses over him as they stole all our stock then rode away up into the mountains. I got shot making for the corral gate. Took my good right leg out from under me. I had to crawl to get to the trough. Got a few shots off hunkered down there, then I got grazed in the head and fell unconscious. A burst of thunder and lightning, then the pain, then the blackness.

"Everything was a-blazing when I came to. Found a couple of blankets hanging on the fence. Got 'em wet and tried to find Pa. Smoke overtook me, and they found me three days later. These good people have been kind enough to care for me until you showed up."

"Show him your back, Shepherd." Sheriff Lyle walked

across the room, standing with his hands on his hips. "You gotta do it, son. He needs to know."

Shepherd looked at Jon and nodded to Sister Donna. " It's ok, Sister. Now may be the best time after all."

Sister Donna unwrapped Shep's back. It was cut and torn, bruised and broken skin crusted over in healing scabs.

"I didn't tell you. Before I got away, they whipped me, Jonny. Just like they did my folks. Tried to hang me, too." He showed the rope burns around his neck. "Mac shot me down before they got him. They'll pay. I'll make them pay."

"Oh my God, Shepherd. The Nolan's did this, too? They killed Pa and burned us out for what happened in Indianapolis? We are going to find these animals. We both will, brother, but you gotta get well first. I'll find them for us."

"They said I deserved it because our pa stood up to them back then. Mac beat the hell out of Whitey that last day. I'd never seen him so mad. I thought Mac was going to kill him, and when Whitey came to his senses, he swore he'd pay him back. We forgot about Indianapolis until they came shooting in the night, like wolves to a blood kill. Took Pa's favorite horse and all the rest of the stock.

"What kind of horses were they?"

"Mixed breeds mostly. All wearing our MCK brand. Most were spotted like the Indian horses they raise farther north. All have been wild since the Spanish came. They have adapted to the climate and the mountains. Good strong spirit and strength. Pa bought a Friesian stallion from a major in the British army up in Vancouver. Paid us a lot of money to train some army horses for them. This one proud stallion, no one could ride. Especially the British Major. He practically gave him to Mac so he would take him away and no one would question the major's horsemanship to his face.

"Mac saw something in this horse. He'd just sit for

hours on the corral rails, talking to him. You know him, he could always tame the wildest, orneriest, cussed, sidewinders in the country. Pa never raised a hand. Just spoke to them. They listened. After a few weeks, I thought I had a new brother. Those two were inseparable. It seemed like they could talk to each other.

"Pa called him Derrygonnally. After an old ghost story he remembered from when he was a kid. It meant ghost or haint. Some type of supernatural devil. That's what Derry was, a black devil if he didn't like you. Them poor devils Whitey has got riding with him are going to get a surprise. Derry wouldn't let anybody ride him, unless it was Mac. He'd bite, kick, and attack you. No one rode him but the old man. Pa was real proud of that."

Jon rubbed his hands together. His face a blank sheet of white with fixed crystal-blue eyes staring ahead, remembering his father's grave and his brother's torn body before him. "I'm going after them, Sheriff Lyle. I won't be able to live with myself if those men go free. Would you introduce me at the bank? I got money to deposit in our name. Shepherd can get the ranch built back up while I find these fellas."

Shepherd tried to get out of bed, but Sister Donna pushed him back down. "Jon, there's a dozen of them at least," he said.

"Shep, I come over the mountains with a wagon train. My friend, Quinn Taylor, is probably the best scout between here and St Louis. Worked me hard and taught me how to live out there. Saved my life as many times as I did his. He's supposed to meet me here in Salem after he is finished with the train. I worked as a teamster, wrangled horses, bulls, mules, and a few good men on that trip. I'm not the schoolboy you remember. We fought Indians, thieves, and bad weather. I'm going after Whitey and his gang as soon as our affairs are in order here."

Jon looked at his brother and the sheriff. "I promised Pa

last night I'd find who killed him. Send Quinn after me when he shows up. Shepherd, between the three of us, Whitey is going to know McKinzey's revenge. We'll have him wearing guts for garters."

Chapter 5

Jon spent the next two days planning and getting ready to leave. Talk around town said the gang would head south for the gold mines so they could quickly sell the horses and scatter. He bought a horse and a mule, supplies, and several boxes of .36 caliber paper cartridges.

Sadly, he said his goodbyes to Shepherd.

"I'll be after you as soon as I can." Shep pushed himself up farther on the bed.

"I'm counting on it, brother. I'm heading south toward the Illinois river. There's a strong strike out there in Gold City. Good market for horses. No one cares which brand they carry."

"Little brother, you watch that temper of yours. You know what a hot head you have. You leave some of those murdering blood thieves for me."

"You get well, Shep. I know you'll come along when you are able. I saw the words on Pa's grave. They were good words."

Jonny rode to his father's grave, after his goodbye to Shepherd. While staying out at the ranch, he made camp close to his father's grave. He'd also spread wildflowers over the grave as he said his goodbyes and shared his plans with Mac, as if he were sitting next to him. He imagined

Mac smoking that old Meerschaum pipe, nodding his head, and exhaling thick white clouds of smoke.

Riding over the ranch brought a deep love and respect for this land he had come to. It was beautiful. Tall virgin forests, crystal-clear running water. Breezes that smelled of pine and spruce swirled around him. There were hardwoods, oaks drooping with acorns. Hickories and walnuts, heavily laden, foretold of a cold winter. The well was deep with sweet water. Grass and wildflowers painted the landscape with abundance, reminding him of paintings he had seen in picture books in school. Game and fish were abundant. His father had picked this land out for them. Three land grants, side by side. He was going to fight to keep it, but first, he had killing to do. A deep pride and determination welled up inside him. He had made a promise and he would keep that promise. If for anything, to heal the hole in his soul.

A cold mist dimmed the day when Jon made his preparations. He'd just finished throwing a diamond hitch over his pack mule when something caught his ear. After tightening the hitch to his liking, he stopped and listened. Hooves clicked in the stones on the lane to the ranch. Standing behind his pack mule, Jon kept low enough he could see whoever approached. His right hand was on the grip of one Navy Colt; the other Colt was tucked into his belt, ready if needed. His heartbeat hammered his temples. No one was going to rob him and get away with it. Not now. Not ever.

"Whoa, ole son. I see you back of that mule. Take your hand off'n that Colt. I'm friendly." Quinn Taylor stepped off of his horse with a huge grin on his face. "I taught you well. You would have had the drop on me if I didn't know you would be ready for any stranger coming up your lane." He stepped forward to shake hands. "I talked to Shepherd and that sheriff. They said you would be out here. I came as fast as I could so I wouldn't miss you. Shepherd was adamant about going, too, but the doc said no and hid his clothes from him." Quinn's eyes shifted toward Mac's stone. "That your pa's grave over there?" He stepped over to the grave, reading the headstone.

Quinn took off his hat and spent a minute paying his respects to John McKinzey. "I didn't know him, Jonny, but I can see, through what you are, that he was a fine man. I'd have been proud to know him. Your brother, Shepherd, is something, too. You told me your story on the trail about your family."

"Did I tell you Shepherd was a fighter? He used to fight the traveling champions when they came to town back in Indianapolis. Shep won most of them. I wish he could be with me now. I miss him. We could always depend on each other." Jonny finished his packing. "I got things to do right now, Quinn. Mean things. I'm not going to be proud of myself when this is over, but I am going to do it. Alone, if I have to. You and Shepherd see to getting the ranch and mill in shape. I'll be back as soon as I am finished."

"Shepherd said you were going after them killers. Brought you something." Quinn walked back to his horse, loosened the ties on the back of his saddle, unrolled a hide he had strapped on the back of his horse, revealing a double-barreled shotgun. "This will help in close quarters. You used this coach gun as a teamster." He tossed it over to Jon. "I pulled it off your wagon so you'd be familiar with it."

Jon held the short double-barreled shotgun, remembering the trip they had shared. "Thanks, I can use this."

"What do you think of me going with you? I'm not much for ranching. Shep knows what needs to be done. I would rather be on the trail of these bushwhackers."

"Quinn, it's personal with me. I gotta do this. It won't be pretty. I've spent the last few days here talking to Pa. I got an ache in my gut that won't be satisfied until they are all accounted for."

"I know. I told ya when I decided to come out and join you and your family that I'd carry my weight. It's a personal grudge with me, too. Besides, you can't talk me out of it."

Jon kicked at a few embers around the dying fire. He squatted and used a rag to pick up the pot and pour a steaming cup. Thoughtfully, he sipped. "Well, seeing as you're all set, I can't turn you down. Care for some coffee before we go? As I recall, you can't cook worth a hoot. Glad you're good with a gun."

Quinn chuckled and knelt next to him. "Coffee always sounds good."

A thunderous clatter of hooves brought both of them to their feet, guns drawn.

Quinn moved into the bushes, gun at the ready, eyes toward the sound.

Shepherd rode into the camp, one leg still wrapped in splints and a bandage on his head. He didn't have any pants on.

"I'm going with you, Jonny. No, you can't talk me out of it. These are the bastards that killed both my families and burned us down. The doctor and the sheriff both tried to talk me out of it, but this murder has been eating at my gut since it happened. Them damn Nolans. I've felt so helpless. I got to go. They were right in front of us. I'm a grown man now, not a child. I'll heal up on the road the rest of the way. I can at least cook. You never was a hand with a skillet. I'm not asking. Quinn, glad to see you here." He stared Jonny down as he walked his horse over to him.

"Here's my hand, brother. Let's go get them son of a bitches together." He held out his hand, and Jonny took it.

"Ya know you ain't got no pants or guns?" Jonny looked up at him. "You got to get some pants on. I ain't gonna listen to you complainin' of saddle sores."

Shepherd slapped his saddlebags. "I'm riding on a

saddle blanket. Had to steal my stuff from the mission. Only had time to pack my guns and a few clothes before they tried to stop me. Can't get my pants on over these splints."

"I guess it's three for revenge after all. We're all packed up. Let's ride."

CHAPTER 6

"Sign says it's New City, Oregon. Don't look like much. Four saloons, a mercantile store, one stable, and, let me count them, six houses, advertising rooms, and women!" Quinn pointed to the mercantile store. "Maybe we can get some supplies from them. It don't seem too promising." He turned back following Shepherd's steady gaze.

Shep's stare was fixed on some horses across the street. "Jon, over there. That black. That's Derry. Something's wrong with him."

They rode forward, stopping behind the horses at the rail to examine their brands—all MCK. Derry had his head down, in an awkward position. Jonny slid off his horse and inspected what was wrong.

"He's got a twitch on his nose, Shep. The meanest thing you can do to a horse. He can't drink. He can't move. Whoa, boy. Easy there." Gently, Jon slid his hand down the horse's neck.

"Be careful, Jon, he doesn't know you." Shep rode a little closer. "Whoa, Derry. Yeah, it's me. That's little Jonny, my brother. He's going to take that twitch off'n you. Easy, Jon." Shep spoke in a whisper, calming Derry to a new hand on him.

25

Jon unwrapped the wire holding the twitch to the rail post then carefully untwisted the wire trap off Derry's nose. "Who done this to you, boy?" Jon flung the twitch onto the boardwalk.

The black head came up, shaking his mane and whistling through his teeth, bellowing his anger and frustration.

Jon slowly stroked his shoulder. "Yes, boy, tell them how much you hate them. You are a McKinzey! It's going to be all right now. Shep and me are here."

Music and laughter came from the saloon to their right.

"Shep, I'm going in there. Stay out here, guarding the horses. I'm going to ask some questions. Quinn, do you mind backing me up?" Jon pulled the coach gun from his saddle then retrieved the twitch. Both Colts were worn military calvary style, butts forward. Jon walked over and watchfully stepped into the darkened Ruby Red saloon.

A redhaired woman, obviously wearing a wig, sang and strutted next to an upright piano, played by a skinny black pianist wearing a river captain's hat and smoking a huge cigar. He happily bounced on the seat, playing a rhythm that was only in his head, as the lady sang another melody with vulgar words and flipped her skirts up, showing her bare thighs occasionally, to keep the attention of their guests and encourage the tips being flicked into a hat on the floor.

Sunshine at one o'clock in the afternoon normally lit up the room. Just this morning, the owner and bartender of the Ruby Red Saloon, Jeff Dower, had screwed brand-new beveled glass windows into the doorframe. Much to his satisfaction, the sun now cast brilliant rays through those bevels, spotlighting his singer and piano player. Red Ruby sang and worked the crowds. Buffing the counter top, Jeff looked up as a shadow crossed his bar, blocking the sun out.

A lonesome cowboy stood in the middle of the room, tapping a twitch against his thigh with his left hand and holding a double-barreled shotgun in the other, ears peeled back, butt of the gun resting on his right thigh, at the ready. The piano player stopped playing as the shadow fell across his music. Ruby raised her fist to him to keep playing, until she saw the man in the middle of the floor. She went quiet, all of her attention focused on the lone man.

Four men in dusters and boots stood at the bar, one foot resting on the brass rail.

"Hey, Moses, why the hell did you quit playin'?" One rounder placed his pipe on the bar then waved his hat to get the piano player's attention.

Moses nodded to the offended rover then nodded toward the man in the center of the room.

The rover turned to look at the lone man standing in silhouette before him. The other compadres turned with him. "Well, what's your story, Jake? What you got there?" He took a thoughtful sip of his beer. "That's my twitch. Did that son of a bitch horse get loose again? He's a strong one, he is. I'll beat him until he falls on the ground."

"Unusual pipe you've got there. A meerschaum, I believe. Only saw one other like it. Did you say that black out there is your horse, mister?" Jon stopped tapping the twitch, letting it fall to the floor.

The drover picked up the pipe, thoughtfully. He moved and rested his hand on one of his pistols. "Yeah, my horse. What's it to ya?" He turned to fire.

Jon shot him in the knee with the right barrel of the coach gun. "Wrong. My horse."

All hell broke loose. The remaining three men dove to the floor for cover, drawing their pistols or grabbing them from the bar.

Quinn shot one of the drovers as he rose to fire at Jon. He stepped from the shadows so everyone could see him, indicating to onlookers to keep out of the fight.

Jon dove toward the redhaired woman, sliding past where she crouched behind the piano. She screamed, picked up her skirts, and fled through the beveled doors, slamming them so hard the glass shattered.

The man Jonny had shot screamed, "I'm bleeding! That son of a bitch shot me. Help!

"Who are you, mister? What do you want?"

A drover with a red garter on his right arm said. "Who the hell are you?"

"The brands on your horses, boys, says those are MCK horses. McKinzey horses. I'm Jonny McKinzey. My pa, Mac, sent me to find you killin' thieves." Jonny pulled his pistol as he rolled away from the piano, firing into the red-gartered man then the one on his right. The first fell into the sawdust on the floor, filling his mouth with tobacco juice and two years of mud and trail dirt. He writhed in pain, clutching his red-gartered left arm. The other leaped over behind a table then slid on his belly behind the bar.

The piano player was no hero; he cowered into a crack in the wall, holding the round swiveled piano seat in front of him, trying not to yell for somebody to come and help him. Small mumblings escaped his lips as he stifled his screams.

Jon fired into the bar. The wounded man on the floor dashed to the door. A shot from outside exploded, and the bloody-faced man fell back into the room.

"Hey, boys, I forgot to tell you, my brother Shepherd McKinzey is outside waiting. Yep, the man you whipped and shot before you burned our ranch down is just outside. He wants to talk to you boys. He's got words for you assholes!" He shot into the bar.

The drover behind the bar stood, grasping his chest with one hand and shooting wildly in the air with the other. He fell forward, tried lifting again to shoot, and Jonny shot him in the throat, leaving him gurgling blood onto the counter.

A deep silence settled over the room.

Jon looked at the man he had shot in the knee. "What is your name, mister?"

Jon dragged a chair over to sit beside the man struggling on the bar floor, retrieving the shotgun before he sat down. He hung his head so he could stare the man directly in his eyes. "What's your name?"

The man kicked his feet around desperately as he tried to crawl away.

Jon fired his pistol into the man's other knee. It blew apart, sending blood and bone into the air, splattering the piano man. A piece of knee landed on his cigar, sizzling it out.

The man howled with pain.

"I said, what is your name?" Jonny broke open the shotgun, extracting the shells, reloading the cartridges, tossing the empties down beside the screaming man's head so he could see them.

"I'm Keith Van Lieu! For God's sakes, mister, what do you want?"

"I'm looking for Whitey Nolan. Know him?" Jon spit down at the bloody mess that was Van Lieu. "Careful how you answer. I've got two new cartridges, and you have only a few more parts I care to shoot. Where is Whitey Nolan?" He pushed the shotgun to the bridge of Keith's nose. "Well? I'm a patient and fair man. Tell me and I'll do the right thing by you."

Keith remained silent, obviously trying to decide what to do. He was dead either way he went, so he thought it best to stall.

"I'll help you decide." Jon picked up the twitch off the floor, tapped it on his leg to knock off any trash. "Let's try this on for size." He straddled the prostrate man and wrapped the twitch around his face. "C'mon, you seem like a strong one. I can do this till your face is cut in two."

Screams filled the room.

Jon backed off the twitch. "Tell me!"

"He went south toward California with the rest of the horses," the man's voice rattled.

Jon removed the twitch.

"He was supposed to meet up with a fella in Wolf Creek, a fella…Jack something…Trapper Jack, yeah that's it. He was going to keep some of the best horses, but especially the mare who was about to foal. Whitey felt she was worth a lot of money. Some of the men who were with him were to stay in Wolf Creek to help out. Whitey was going on from there to sell the rest of horses all at once in Gold City, another mining town."

"How'd you get the black?" The shotgun cut into the bridge of Van Lieu's nose.

"No one else could ride him. The boss hated him 'cause he couldn't ride him. I got him as part of my divvies up. I thought I could beat him down, but I can't ride him much, neither, not without the twitch. No one can, I guess. He's the meanest damn horse I ever seen."

"Mac McKinzey could."

The man looked up. "What?"

"My pa was Mac McKinzey."

"Mr. McKinzey, you said you'd treat me fair if I tol' ya where Whitey was." He attempted a smile, showing his teeth.

"That's what I said." Jon shot him in the face with both barrels. "That's fair."

Piano man had been watching close when the skull bones and brain sprayed him in the face. He went pale, retching his stomach clean into his captain's hat then spat the offal from his mouth.

"We're done here, Quinn." Jon picked up the pipe from the bar and placed it in his pocket, leaving the saloon without a backward glance.

Red Ruby screamed as he came through the door, pulling up her skirts before running back in the saloon looking for Jeff.

Jon walked over to Derry, whispering to him softly, attempting to stroke him, but the stallion shied away. Finally, after more coaxing, Derry allowed Jon to put his hand on him, patting his neck, letting him smell his body as he got closer.

Shepherd shook his head in wonder. "I'll be damned. You are Mac's son all right."

"I got this off of one of them." He handed the pipe to Shep.

"Mac's pipe. I'll be damned."

Jon didn't try to mount Derry, but he took the reins and led him away from the hitching post. "I'll take him."

They rode over to the feed store. Quinn got down. Jon passed a list to him and gave him some money. Quinn took the money, stuffed it into his vest pocket. He climbed up the steps to the sidewalk before turning around to survey the town for trouble. Satisfied all was clear, he entered the store.

"I'm looking for .36 caliber paper shells, ten-gauge shells, five pounds of beef jerky, a side of bacon, twelve cans of beans, peaches, and corn, five pounds of flour and coffee, and three dollars of penny candy." He handed the list to a cowering store clerk.

They divided the goods up between their saddlebags then turned away from the store. No one in the town approached them as they rode out, heading south. Jon led Derry. Shep led the other three horses with MCK brands.

CHAPTER 7

Indianapolis 1843

Mac stepped away from the desk. "Ya mean you won't do nuthin' about it. Those people was murdered out there." He slapped both hands on the desk. "Damn it, Griff, we go a long ways back. I expected more from you."

Griffin Ashford pushed away from his desk. "I'm sorry, Mac. I'm sheriff of the town. I ain't got no jurisdiction out in the country outside city limits. I will call in the marshals to look into it, but you know them Jaspers will be long gone by the time they get here. Besides, all you got to go on is the word of that ten-year-old kid. A nigger kid at that. Ain't much to go on. You know that."

"I'll let that remark pass, Griff, 'cause I've know you so long. Don't ever say it to me again." He stopped, hard eyes surveying the sheriff.

"I'm sorry, Mac, but that is the way of it. I won't repeat it again in your presence. I understand how you feel about that boy."

"Shepherd said one of the men had a shock of white hair. His mask didn't cover his head. That man is Whitey Nolan. That's enough for me, Griff. Those Nolan's have been braggin' how they chase down escaped slaves and take 'em back south, ever since they come up from Arkansas. They're over at the stables now, getting a new rim on their wagon. I saw them as I came in."

"They've got the right to move about as they please, Mac. It's a free country."

"For some folks it is." Mac let the silence descend between them. "I'll see you later, Griff."

Mac stepped out of the office, shutting the door behind him loudly. He felt defeated by his friend's indifference to what had happened to the Bienville's. A lot of citizens in town felt the same way, he knew.

Mac heard a loud voice. A crowd gathered down at the stable. Whitey Nolan stood in the back of a wagon, beseeching passersby to let him know if they were any more runaways in town, anyone they knew about.

Mac McKinzey was five foot seven, weighing one hundred and sixty-five pounds. He wasn't a big man, but years of handling horses and breaking them had whittled any fat from his frame. Mac was all sinew and muscle. His jaw involuntarily clenched as Whitey talked.

He didn't know when he started walking toward Whitey with a steady purposeful gait. Grim determination froze his face. No thoughts crossed his mind except a deepening anger that grew with each step.

"Whitey Nolan. I'm calling you a murderin', low-life bastard. You burned down those folks house and hung them like they were animals. I know ya done it and your murderin' brothers, Lucky and Steve." He gestured to the crowd. "Is this the kind of trash you want in our town? A sneaking gang of murderers, hiding behind masks under the false guise of legalities?"

Whitey jumped from the wagon. He had a shock of white hair on the right side of his head, which stood out from his thick dark hair. Standing over Mac a good six inches, he outweighed him by forty pounds. He looked around to see who was listening. "Now hold on there. Who are you anyway? What gives you any right to say those words to me?"

"The right of any decent folk who know what murderers and black-hearted scum will do to defenseless people if we let it happen."

"What 'happening' are you talking about?" He checked his audience again, to see who was watching. He stepped forward. "Are you calling us murderers and scum to my face? That's what I'm hearing."

"You murdered the Bienville's. The black family down the hill from me. I found them hanged, shot, their home burning down." Mac spat to the ground.

He turned to the crowd. "I seen dem poor people hanging by their necks. Their only sin was that God made 'em darker than us. Call yourselves Christian and abide innocent people hung like meat? Is that how you want to live?"

No one in the crowd muttered a word. Most hung their heads or cast their eyes down at the ground.

Pointing to Whitey, he said, "Their son identified you to me as a man with a shock of white hair. Where's your mask, you cowardly dog? You've been here for weeks stirring it up about runaway slaves. The Bienville's were freemen."

"They had a son?" Whitey bit his lip. "Don't know what you are talking about, mister. So what, if some Negras got burned out! No one cares. I don't care. Now keep your big mouth shut, or I'll make you sorry you accused me of anything. I'll whip you in front of all these people here and now." Whitey stuck a big finger into Mac's chest. A belligerent smile creased his face.

Mac grabbed the hand and finger with his strong right hand and held it so Whitey couldn't draw it back. No one broke Mac McKinzey's iron grip. Whitey's grin faded.

"I'll teach you, little man!" Whitey pushed Mac with a

powerful left arm, freeing up his right hand. He swung it at Mac's face.

Mac blocked it with his left arm, stepped into Whitey, and delivered a right to Whitey's mouth. "Damn you to hell, Nolan."

Whitey stepped back, surprised by the solid punch he just received. "I'll make you sorry you did that, John McKinzey." He grabbed the front of Mac's shirt, pulling him close then smashed his right fist into his face, knocking him down.

Mac shook the punch off, got to his feet, came up under Whitey with an uppercut to his stomach then a left cross to his chin. He put him on the ground with a follow-up right cross to his nose.

Whitey fell to his knees, his busted nose bleeding and swelling. It looked like a red pickle lying across his face. Charging like a bull, he pile-drived the smaller man back into the wagon with his head. Holding him against the wagon with his left hand, Whitey rained punch after punch into Mac's face.

Mac dropped to the ground, grabbing Whitey's legs. Twisting hard, he dumped Whitey into the dirt of the street. Grabbing his hair, Mac lifted Whitey's face and smashed another powerful punch into his nose. He stood.

"Get up, you snake. This little man isn't done with you." He let Whitey climb to his feet.

Whitey touched his swelling nose. "All right, you got the best of me." Smiling, he stepped forward offering to shake hands.

Mac didn't move, crouched to fight; he was ready when Whitey charged him. He stepped to the side as Whitey blindly flailed by. Mac tripped him. Whitey fell back onto the street next to the horse trough.

"That trick never works. Never trust a liar."

Yelling with rage, Whitey charged again, stopping in front of Mac this time, throwing a fist into his right shoulder. Mac blocked it and swung with his right. The big man ducked just in time then whipped a left hand to connect to McKinzey's chin. It stunned Mac. His knees wobbled. Whitey hurried to follow through, repeating a left into Mac's face, knocking him down.

Whitey kicked dust with his left leg. John caught the leg and pushed it over his head, sprawling Whitey onto the street again. Both men rolled over, coming up swinging. The two men traded punch for punch until Mac delivered a ground-to-sky uppercut, throwing Whitey's head back. The big man stood for a moment on his toes, blinking into the sun, trying to maintain his balance. His eyes blanked out then he collapsed face down onto the street, like a wet blanket.

"That's enough." Lucky Nolan pulled his pistol. He moved over, grabbing Mac from behind around his neck. "Let's see if you can beat this?" He pushed his barrel into Mac's neck.

"Drop it, Lucky." Sheriff Griff had been hidden by the crowd. He stepped through, pointing his shotgun at Whitey's brother. Searching the crowd, he shouted, "Steve Nolan. You move over where I can see you both." He waited until Steve stepped out of the stable and joined his brother.

"Drop your pistol, Lucky. I'll not say it again." He moved closer to Lucky and John, a stern look on his face.

Lucky watched Griff. He slowly shook his head no and licked his lips, nervously glancing side to side and all around for any support from the crowd.

Moving fast for a big man, Griff surprised Lucky when he wacked the man's skull with both barrels of the shot gun, creasing his forehead. Lucky grunted as he eyes rolled back, and he crumpled where he stood.

"This will not happen in my town." He barked at Steve. "You're the oldest. Haul these boys out of here, or I'll throw you all in jail. I'd hold you until the marshals get here, but they're not due for about ten days. I want you out of here, now!"

Steve nodded. Gesturing for some of the crowd to help him, they put the fallen brothers in the wagon.

Mac dusted off his pants then sucked at his knuckles.

Steve yelled at him, "We won't forget this, McKinzey. We won't ever forget. You'll never see us coming, but one of these days, our paths will cross again. Tell that kid we'll be back for him, too!" He bellowed at his team and skidded the wagon out of town.

Mac wiped his mouth with the back of his hand, watching the Nolan's leave town.

Griff came over to see how he was. "Getting mighty old ta be fighting in the streets. You need to see Doc."

"So, you saw what happened. You know you could have stopped it all along, Griff."

"I know, Mac. I simply wanted to watch you beat the hell out of Whitey Nolan. I owed you that."

CHAPTER 8

Oregon Territory, 1853

Quinn was worried. These were not the carefree, eager young men he remembered. John's death weighed heavily on both brothers.. Quinn had lost family and friends. He remembered what it was like. This was something different. The kid was losing weight. Shepherd, all nerves, distant, distracted. They rode all day. Not a word passed between them. Quinn would call them to their meals.

Jon ate then either he would go off practicing with his gun, or he would fuss and curry Derry, sometimes working with him on a lead. The pair grew close.

Shepherd still only hobbled, and they had to cut a branch for him so he could get around. He watched how Jonny and Derry were getting along. Derry surprised him, as Jon built a new level of confidence between them so quickly. Normally, he would only tolerate Shepherd and Mac, but only Mac could mount and not be unseated.

"I'm a little bit jealous you and Derry are hitting it off so well." Shepherd offered Jon a cup of coffee then poured a little whiskey in it. "Let's talk."

Jon tethered Derry to their picket line. He took the cup

offered. "To you, brother. We haven't had a drink together in over two years."

Both drank then grew quiet in their thoughts.

"You remind me of Pa so much. You got Mac's touch with horses, all right. He taught me everything he knew, but I don't have the touch. You and Mac do."

"Shep, Derry is amazing. Taking that twitch off his lip earned me some trust, I guess. I hardly have to think of something and he is doing it. Sorry if you're jealous. I just can't help it." He sat on the log next to Shepherd. "I can't get Pa out of my mind."

"Me, too, Jon. I want to get this business done and over with. The sooner the better." Shep poured a little more whiskey in his cup. "Oh, maybe jealous is too strong a word. How about envious? I'm proud, too. Knowing that my little brother came across that great wilderness on his own and is right beside me makes my heart prideful."

Quinn joined them. "I'd like a taste of your whiskey, Shep." He saluted both of them. "Good to hear you boys talkin'. You've had me worried. Ya know, Shep, your brother and I came across on the wagon train together. He can carry his own weight. Any man on the train would have no problem riding the river with Jonny. Did he tell you about becoming a blood brother to the Shoshone? It was at Bridger's Fort. He got into a wrestling match with a young buck. What was his name, Jonny?"

Jonny paused a little. "Don't go telling any tales on me, Quinn. You can stretch the truth farther than I can throw."

"Well, this ain't one of those times. C'mon, what was his name? I know you was sweet on his sister."

"Sister?" Shep shifted his attention to his younger brother. "You met an Indian girl? You did grow up on the trail. Well give, what were their names?"

"Her name was, or is, Laughing Grass, her brother is Little Bear. Little Bear and I wrestled in some of their games. Neither of us won. We just quit because we got so exhausted we couldn't move. I held his hand up for victory. He held my hand up. We were both lying on the ground. They had to help us to our feet. Flying Eagle, his father and spiritual healer in the tribe, invited me to become blood brothers with Little Bear because they admired my courage and stamina. That's how Little Bear got his name. No one could outwrestle him. Flying Eagle said I showed Shoshone strength and courage. I wouldn't quit. Here's the scar." Jonny took off his glove, showing a livid white scar across his hand.

"And this Laughing Grass? Where does she come in?"

Quinn butted in. "That night at the feast, this certain girl, a very shapely girl, danced in front of Jon all night. Seems no matter where the rest of the dancers moved to, Laughing Grass was always swaying herself in front of Jonny boy, there." He grinned. "He didn't take his eyes off her all night."

"Little Bear grew embarrassed. He asked his mother, Quiet Woman, to tell her to stop. She wouldn't do it. Her parents liked me, it seems. I hope to go back and see them one of these days. She gave me this." Jon lifted a leather thong from around his neck, attached was a length of blue ribbon. "She wore it in her hair at the feast."

"Oh, little brother. Is that all there is to the story?" He raised his eyebrows suspiciously at Jon.

"Shep! That's all that happened. I became friends with the tribe. She gave me a token so I wouldn't forget."

"That and that scar on your hand." Shep chuckled then finished his drink.

The evening quieted down as the sun sank over the darkening western horizon. A cool breeze wafted over them as shadows deepened. Frogs croaked out love songs from deep haunts in wet grasses and ponds. Crickets sang their songs from logs and hidden places. The men sat in thought, each unto themselves.

Quinn broke the silence. "I know your pa's death weighs

heavy on your minds, but I got a stake in this, too. Any idea where we're headed?"

"A place called Wolf Creek, from what Van Lieu said back in the saloon. That would be a good place to hang out, try to sell horses to pilgrims and those on the Owl Hoot Trail. Maybe to miners needing an extra horse. Besides, the four we have, I guess there are maybe two dozen more. One of the spotted mares was in foal. She should have had her baby or be due right soon. They'd have to keep her safe or lose the baby if they are any horsemen at all." Shepherd painfully got up, holding his hip. "Got to get some sleep, if I can. We gots lots of road before us. See you in the morning."

Shep dropped into his blankets, pulling them over his shoulder, turning his back to them. He used both arms to position his leg so he could get comfortable.

Quinn said, "He ain't doing so good. The riding isn't helping the leg, and he doesn't get much sleep from the pain. He refuses to take the laudanum. Says he can't ride with it, and he sure as hell can't hit anything he is shooting at. I'm worried about him."

"I've seen it, too. Big brother is his own man, but I think this trail is too much for him right now. He is his own man, and nothing I can say is going to deter him. Pa's death plays on my mind. Shep's, too. You and I have been on the trail together for a long time. I owe everything I know about staying alive out here to you. Glad you're with us, Quinn. Guess I'll go hit my blankets, too." Jon walked off into the dark toward his bed.

Quinn sat by the fire, staring into the embers, wondering what would become of all of this. "We can only guess what the future may hold, but by damn, we are rushing off to find it. I think I read that somewhere."

Feeling very alone, he poured his drink into the fire, causing it to flare up, sending sparks heavenward.

That was how it went until they got to Wolf Creek. This

was a tiny little town nestled in the mountains of the lower Cascades on the new Applegate Trail as it cut through the southwest half of the Oregon Territory. Here it turned north toward the Willamette River to Salem and Portland, continuing until it reached the Columbian River Gorge. Huge old-growth oaks, pines, and spruce covered the mountains, creating a fresh fragrance of woodland perfume mixed with the loamy richness of the earth and deep forest. Water was abundant in the many springs and creeks that gushed from the mountainsides, gurgling into placid pools, alive with fish.

In Wolf Creek, they tied their horses in front of a large white store with tall columns supporting a second-floor balcony. It must have been a grand home at one time but was seeing poorer days now. This building sat across and above a rushing stream tumbling over rocks and boulders channeling the freshet as it oozed out of the mountain's side.

"Fellas, stay with the horses." Jon dismounted, stopping to rub Derry's nose. It had healed up quickly under Jon's care.

"You be careful in there, little brother. Don't know what might happen if you ask too many questions."

"What is it, Shep? Speak up! I can't hear you for that stream. Makes a lot of noise."

Quinn stood up in his stirrups. "He said..." but he realized Jon couldn't hear either of them for the cascading stream across from the inn. He simply waved him on.

Jon had already turned his back and climbed the steps to the large porch surrounding the inn. Shep sat in resignation, spitting into the dust. Digging a braid of tobacco out of his pocket, he muttered as he chewed and worked on it then stuffed the wad in his mouth. Crossing his arms over his chest, he chomped his frustration out on his new chew, spitting when he must, until the cud fit comfortable in his jaw and a feeling of ease washed up his body.

Millicent Ortego glanced up at the handsome stranger who came through the door. He had obviously been on the road, but he was neat with his hair combed back. Tall in his boots, broad across the shoulders, he would have caught her eye if she had been a single woman. Now, she found herself mildly aroused as he quietly came across the room, holding her transfixed by his steel-gray eyes. Irritated by the feelings that welled within her, she cleared her throat and dropped the ledger she had been working on. A flush filled her cheeks, the predicament embarrassing her altogether.

"Ma'am." He tipped his hat then appraised the goods for sale.

"Yes," she said shrilly, from under the desk. Rising, she pulled at her hair. "What can I do for you?"

"I'm a stranger in these parts. Heard tell of a fella with a white shock of hair in his scalp. His friends, I believe, call him Whitey. Might've passed through this way. Maybe he stopped here and bought supplies? He left some of those horses with a man who has a ranch close by? Well, anyway, I heard he may have some horses for sale. Would you know this man? I'm looking to find him and the horses."

"I, er, ahem," she muttered, trying to clear her throat. She pointed to the back room. "Mr. Ortega," she called out. "Man." Her voice broke again. "Man, here to see you."

"Yes, Millie dear. What is it?" Manuel Ortega, stepped out of the back office, wiping his mouth with a green linen towel. He stopped when he saw the stranger.

"He'll know," Millie blurted out, nodding toward him. "Excuse me." She blushed at her discomfort and left the room under the eyes of the stranger and her husband.

"Oola. That's strange. What come over with her?" Manuel stared at her retreating back until the door closed a little bit too loudly. "I wonder? Women is sometimes the strangest acting…creatures. I don always know what to think like dem. You been married, *amigo*?" Manuel rolled his eyes.

"No. No, I haven't."

Manuel put down his towel, not sure why he was called. "What do you need? Millie didn't tell me nothing."

"I'd like five pounds of Arbuckle's, a flitch of bacon, and some of those canned goods I see over there. I'm also searching for a family of brothers named Nolan. He is supposed to have passed through these parts, driving some horses. Perhaps several weeks ago? Maybe he left some of the horses. A red-and-white paint mare for instance with a local rancher? Know of anybody that fits that bill?"

"I seen this man. Got a white knot of hair on da side of his head. I saw hem, about a month ago. Yes, hem and others was driving some horses, trying to find buyers." Manuel rolled his eyes again. "If you ain't too par-tic-u-lar, where dey come from? He went south with most of the herd, the res, dey went north with one of the drovers who was with hem. Dat Trapper Jack, he is called. A very bad man. He got a lot of udder men who came down wit da fella wit da white knot, stay up der wit him. He got a ranch up der. Jusa minute." He returned with the coffee and bacon. "Whad ones you want with da cans, *señor*?"

Satisfied he had found his man, Jon pointed to some peaches, peas, and potatoes. He studied the selection then decided on a couple of cans of tomatoes to finish his order. "What's this drover's name again? Jack? Maybe, he'll sell me some of those horses."

"He is called, Trapper Jack, if dat is his real name? You never know who is or who is not aroun' here. Do you know what I am saying?"

Jon nodded. "How do I find this Trapper Jack. I want to see those horses."

"You sure? Well, okay. I see you mean to go. Go north on the road outside da store here. It follow Wolf Creek about five mile. Take da firs road to da left. Jack's place is first lane on da right, about another two ta three miles. Only ranch out thata way. Not many folks go out there. Good place to stay away from." He rolled his eyes again.

"I'll keep that in mind."

"Did you hear me say dey is probably stolen horses?"

"I'm counting on it. You see, they are my horses."

Manuel stopped what he was going to say, leaving his mouth open. He placed the order in a gunny sack and pushed it across the counter to Jon. He appraised the young stranger with a different eye than before. Jon paid for the food and turned to go.

Millie peeked out the door.

Jon tipped his hat. "Thank you, ma'am."

"Your horses! You don't say dat before!" Manuel Ortega appealed to the tall young man. "Be careful out thata way, *amigo*. Trapper Jack, he hang around wit a mean crowd of thieves."

Jon closed the door.

"Nice fella, though he don't buy much. Hope he'll be alright out there. Good-looking young fella, too, don't ya think, Millie?"

"I didn't pay any attention, Manuel. I got a store to run. I don't have time to be gazing at strangers. I hope he gets his horses back." She glanced out the window and saw the trio ride away. "He's got some help at least."

CHAPTER 9

"**H**ey, Trapper. Man out here wants to look over your horses. Said he's willing to buy them all, if'n they is of sound stock. Seems kinda young, more like a kid to me. Bet he ain't got no money. Probably jus' achin' for a hobby horse to ride." Manny guffawed and the rest of the bunkhouse joined in.

"How'd he get in here without any of us seein' him?" Trapper wasn't happy, kid or no kid. "Any of you see him ride in? We don't get trespassers up this way." Everyone shrugged. No one had seen the rider come up the lane or any other approach to the house. "Where is he?" Trapper Jack moved to the door to see the young stranger talking to the horses.

"Why, he's out at the corral, throwing kisses to the horses. Standing out there as plain as day, when I came out of the outhouse this morning. Thought you knowed about it."

"Okay, Manny. I'll see to our visitor. You fellas just hang out on the porch in case I need you. I'll find out who this galoot is." Trapper opened the door of the bunkhouse. He stopped to roll a cigarette as he studied the man at the corral.

His leathery face bespoke of years of rough living.

Something with this kid seemed wrong. Trapper took his time checking around to see if there was anyone with this boy. After drawing deeply, he exhaled. Smoke covered his face, hiding it for a moment. Suddenly, he threw away his unfinished smoke, striding forward to challenge the stranger. "Hey, you. What are you doing here?" He rested his hands on his gun belt. "I said, who are you?"

Jon turned away from the corral and surveyed Trapper with an innocent smile on his face. "As you can see, just looking at your fine horses here. Man back a piece said you had some for sale. Bring me a cup of coffee when you come out. I could use a cup just now." He turned back to the corral, talking to the horses. "Nice red-spotted mare over there in the far pen. Colt appears to be pretty new. Hurry with that coffee, will you?"

"Coffee! Who does this fella think he is?" Trapper started forward but was stopped midstride by the stranger's demand. He hesitated then gestured to Manny. "Bring me a cup of coffee. I'll pour it down his throat."

Manny was caught off guard. He was no servant and opened his mouth to say so, but mindful of Trapper's temper, he thought better about complaining, and stomped off for the coffee. He came back, a steaming tin cup in his gloved hand, and passed it to his boss. "I got it almost boilin'."

Trapper let a scowl cross his face as he marched toward the corral. "I got your coffee, bub. Who was this man told you I had horses for sale? It had better be the right name, or you're goin' to wear this coffee, and it's going to run out of your gullet from the bullet I put in your belly."

"Let me see now." Jon took the coffee from Trapper, blowing on it a bit as he had seen the steam rolling off the top. After slurping it, he smacked his lips. "Hmmm. Good coffee, thanks. Seems to me… What was his name? Oh, yes. Called hisself Keith…Keith Van Lieu, as I remember. Had a few friends with him."

"Van Lieu, huh? Where did you meet this Van Lieu?" Trapper placed his hand on his pistol.

"We met in New City, at a saloon there. He had three other fellas with him. He also had a fine Friesian stallion. Said a Whitey Nolan had been running some horses south to the gold fields and was coming through Wolf Creek. That's why I came here. Said the best of the horses would be left with a Trapper Jack. Does Van Lieu sound like someone you know?" Jon offered a friendly smile and turned his back to Trapper. "Yes, sir, that mare is a beauty."

"So, Van Lieu is blabbering his mouth off about me. He say anything else?" Trapper cut a chew and stood beside Jon, looking at the horses, chomping with vigor, before he spat into the corral.

"No not much. I stopped and spoke to the man who owns the store in town. Has a pretty wife by the way. Said a man fitting my description of Whitey came through there about a month ago with horses and left some of them at a ranch run by a Trapper Jack. Ring a bell with you?"

"Manuel said that did he? That Mex was shootin' his mouth off about my horses, was he? He shoulda knowed better than that."

"He meant no harm. He was just trying to help me out. I was interested in the horses Whitey Nolan had. Manuel said you took some to your ranch. I came by to see them. I'm a buyer. So?"

"So, what?"

"You got horses to sell or not? I like what I see here. How about the mare?"

"Mare and colt ain't for sale, but I'll give you a good price for the rest." Turning back to the porch, he addressed his men. "You can all stand down. That Mex in town, Manuel, sent him. Go about your duties. Smitty, go bring in those horses in the pasture. Maybe our friend here would like to look-see them, too. What was your name, friend?"

"Interesting brands on these animals. MCK. Your brand?"

"Naw. I just got 'em recently. Come from up north a piece. Didn't catch your name?"

Jon waved his hand toward the corral. "What's your price for all of these horses in the corral and the mare and foal?"

"I told ya. The mare and foal ain't for sale."

"That's a shame. Seems like he is getting about pretty spry. Would you call him a yellow horse with red spots or a red horse with yellow spots?"

"Yeah, he's coming along. Bred from good stock. His mama is a beauty. Three hundred dollars and you can have the whole lot. They're the best horses in the territory. Anybody will tell you that, but not the mare and foal, they're worth that, and more."

"Don't you think that's a little steep?" Jon glanced at the porch. All the men had gone about their duties.

"What ya mean steep? Them's all fine stock. Pretty fancy horses for these parts. Hey. Who are you anyway?"

"Maybe you heard of me. They call me Jonny Mac."

"Mac? No, can't say that I have. So, you interested or not?"

"Perhaps this will clear it up for you. Mac is short for McKinzey. Ever heard of John McKinzey? I'm Jonny McKinzey, of the MCK brand." Jon stepped close to Trapper as he finished.

"McKinzey! Why you…"

Trapper went for his gun, but Jon was too close to him. He had his hand on Trapper's gun hand, forcing it snug in his belt. Jon had already drawn and pulled Trapper onto the barrel of the Navy Colt with his left hand before blasting his belly point-blank with the right.

The gun blast deafened Trapper's surprised scream.

Jon leaned Trapper up against a corral post behind a lilac bush, like they were still looking at the horses. He shot again into a tree close by and turned to see men poking their heads out of the barn and bunkhouse. Jon waved his gun at them.

"Sorry! Just showing Trapper my new gun. Navy Colt." He waved the gun in the air.

The men, reassured, went back to their work.

Jon put his arm around the moaning white-faced Trapper Jack. "I'll take all of your horses, Trapper. Thanks. That's a great deal." Leaning closer, he whispered in his ear. "Where is Whitey and the rest of them Nolans? Tell me and I'll make it fast. Don't say anything and you'll lie around here for days, gut shot while the gangrene slowly rots you, bit by painful bit. You'll smell the stench of your own meat falling off your bones. No help, no relief, no matter how loud you scream. Now, tell me where they are."

"My boys will kill you for this. Real slow, too."

"That's my worry." Jon jabbed his gun deeper into Trapper's ribs. "Where's them Nolans?"

"Aoww!" Trapper screeched. "Whitey, his brothers, and a few other men was headed for the gold fields on the Illinois River. A place called Gold City. The rest of the stock are with him."

"Give me some names, Trapper. I want their names."

"There's just one name I know, McKinzey, 'sides them Nolans. Damn you. My guts are killing me. They're falling out for god's sake!"

"Give me a name, Trapper," hissed Jon through clenched teeth, checking his back to make sure no one was on the porch. "Give me a name and I'll end it."

"One of them is a Winfro. You know how it is. No one gives their real name. He's a young kid too mean to live to an old age. Full of hisself. Diamond Winfro, yeah, that's what he called himself. Another fella is older. Never heard his name. Carried a shotgun. There's more, but that's all I know. They're waitin' fo' me..."

"Be waitin' for Whitey. In hell, Trapper!" Jon fired

again into the dying man's body and jammed him tighter onto the corral fence, wedging him up against a post and rail, so it appeared he was still talking about the horses.

Jon swung the gate open, whistling a tune that had come into his head from the riverboat, "Oh Susanna." Still whistling, he walked to his horse and mounted. He rode into the corral and gathered the horses at one end. Leaning over the far gate, he released the spotted mare and the colt from their pen. With a sharp whistle, he moved the horses out toward the lane and down the road.

He waved his hat at Trapper as he passed. "Nice doing business with you, Trapper Jack."

Jon gave another sharp whistle and a "Hurrah, move up there!" He kicked his mount into a trot and then a full gallop, driving the horses ahead of him.

Smitty brought in a group of six horses and drove them into the corral. After closing the gate behind him with one hand, he rode over to Trapper. "Here ya go, Jack, six more. Where's the kid who come for the horses? Where's all the horses? Boss?"

Smitty dismounted and put his hand on Trapper's shoulder. Trapper's body crumpled to the ground. Lifeless eyes stared up into the face of a now-pale Smitty.

Trapper was already enjoying the delights in the pits of hell.

The first shot pricked up every man's ears, but they thought the buyer was still showing off. The second and third one, in rapid succession, brought everybody running.

"Trapper Jack has been killed," Smitty hollered at everyone. "Gun is still in his holster. All the horses is gone. Anybody seen anything?"

Everybody shook their heads.

"Mount up. We're riding after that no-account murdering buzzard. Meet up at the gate."

Smitty stood up in his stirrups, waiting for everyone to gather. "Let's go get that gut-shooting, horse-stealing, sneaky coyote!" Smitty turned his horse, kicked its belly, and led them down the lane at full gallop.

The men followed, their hats blown back behind their heads. Grim determination etched across their faces. Trapper Jack wasn't much, but he had been one of them, and they were honor bound to go after the *hombre* that gut shot him.

Quinn's Sharps rifle boomed. Smitty flipped over the back of his horse, falling underneath the sorrel mare behind him, fracturing her right front leg and causing her to crash to the ground, pitching the rider, Stan Bennett, over her back. He hit hard, shattering his neck as he skidded across the rocky ground. The young horse rolled and kicked in the road, shrieking her fear and pain.

"He, hee, he! C'mon boys! I can pick you all off from here, one at a time." Quinn's excited voice challenged them to keep coming. He shot another round at their feet. Quinn was hidden, high up on a ridge where they couldn't see him. "Them horses was stolen anyways. You want to all get killed over a few stolen horses?"

Manny pulled up, looking up in the rocks for the shooter but couldn't find him. There was a single cloud of gun smoke drifting over the face of the green tangle of brush fronting the rocky ledge. Nothing else gave away the location of the rifleman. He could be anywhere on the rock face. They would get picked off one at a time, like turkeys roosting on a limb.

"Whoa, boys. Whoa." He cautioned the men as they pulled up then turned his horse to face them. "Sharps will leave a pretty big hole in you. I liked Trapper. You all knowed that. He always treated me good. How about you boys? Them was stolen horses, ya know. The Nolans stolen horses. I guess they ain't worth getting killed over." He nodded to two of the riders. "You fellas go find Smitty's horse."

Stan's horse screamed its pain, calling for their

attention. "We'll stay here and pick up what's left of Smitty and Stan and put down Stan's horse. *Damn, I'll have to tell Stan's old lady about this, too. She'll be real broke up.* Manny stood up in his stirrups and waved his hat in the air at Quinn then slid off his horse, hands up.

"They's backing down, Jonny. See at 'em, movin' off like the belly-crawlin' snakes they is." Quinn fired a round into the ground just to see them jump.

"They don't want to get killed, any more than anyone else, for nothin'." Jon watched the men pick up the bodies of their dead friends. "Time for us to go."

"Where do we go from here? What are we goin' to do with all the horses? The mare looks good. Mac named her Mary. That colt beside her is spry and healthy, but we'll have to take time on the trail for him. He ain't strong yet. Too little. What about that, Jon? Have you thought about that?" Shep squinted at Jon. He wondered what his little brother would do. Did they both have what it took to finish this?

This was the second time they had faced Whitey's gang. Jon had killed up close, deliberately, without mercy or rancor again. His clothes and hands were bloody from it. Shepherd had killed his man in the fight. Quinn had drawn blood at the bar and, just now, two more. It could change a man. He knew, it may turn them all into outlaws, outside society's norms. Maybe, with the horses to take care of, Jon would stop now.

Jon didn't hesitate. "We part here, friend and brother. I can make faster time alone. You get the horses back to the ranch, won't you? There's too many to come with us. Hire someone to help you if you need to. Shepherd, you are no good on the trail. You'll slow me up. That leaves Quinn to get all of you back to the ranch. Derry is strong enough to travel. He's going with me. You keep the pack horses. I'm taking just what I need."

"Look, little brother, when did you start telling me what to do?" Shep threw his injured leg over his saddle and slid off, coming down on one good leg. "I'm going, too. No one, not even you, is telling me what I'm doing."

"Okay, big brother, let's have it out right here. Quinn, you'll fall in with whoever wins?"

Quinn took off his hat, shielding his face a little. "Oh hell. I guess so. I'm part of all this."

Jon pulled on his gloves as he walked up to Shepherd. Shep tried to push him back, but Jon slipped under the push and shoved Shepherd to the ground with both hands.

"That was no fair. Jonny, damn it, you tricked me." Shep struggled to get up, but without his stick, he was helpless. "Get me up."

"Get up yourself. Sorry, big brother, but you're going to get one of us killed. See to the ranch, be able to ride and shoot, and come find me when you're well. I'll leave a big enough trail even a child could follow it."

Jon took the saddle off his horse and put it on Derry's back. The big stallion immediately perked up. After filling saddlebags with food and a sleeping roll, Jon checked his canteen and ammunition. Turning to his brother and Quinn, he offered his hand. "I know this ain't been like our other trips, Quinn, but I was mighty grateful for what you did. If I live through this, I'll see you both back at the ranch. Big brother, see you down the trail. If not..." Jon touched his hat in goodbye. "Let's just leave it at *adios*."

Jonny walked to Derry, talking soothingly and stroking his neck. He pulled the stallion's face up to his and blew into the horse's nostrils. Derry shook his head then nudged his shoulder.

Jon moved to the side, still stroking the big black. Easy like, he stepped lightly into the saddle. Derry stood for a moment, feeling Jon on his back. He snorted, coming to attention. Jon gave him a gentle kick with his heels, and they moved off.

"I'll be damned. Just like Pa." Shep marveled at what he had just witnessed.

Aboard the now-invigorated Derry, Jon looked at his brother with a drawn and lean face. He fought to stay in the saddle as Derry sidestepped, feeling frisky and ready to go. "Remember what I done. I ain't proud of it, but I'm not ashamed, either. It needed doing. I promised Pa. I'd kill them all. Come find me, you two. I'll be watching for you. We'll finish it together."

Jon gave a sharp whistle to an excited Derry, saluted Shep and Quinn, and turned down the trail, galloping away. The clouds of dust swallowed him up from behind.

Quinn had no words. He watched the haggard young man ride away. Guiltily, he was glad, but he had deep fearful feelings about how this would turn out. Once a man goes over the edge, the killing becomes a reflex. They were like a wounded old boar bear, killing anything that gets in their way.

"C'mon, Shepherd. Let's get you on your feet." Quinn gave the walking stick to Shep then he helped haul him to a standing position.

"Damn it, Quinn. Damn it to hell. I know Jonny is right. I jus' didn't want him to face them killers alone. I lost Mac. I don't know what I would do if I lost Jon. I jus' don' know what I would do."

CHAPTER 10

Quinn beat the dust from his pants. "My daddy used to say, 'If you're going someplace, you'd better get started.' You up for this, Shep? We gotta move these horses before those fellas change their minds. There are a lot more of them than the two of us."

Shep watched until the last of his brother's form disappeared from sight then he wiped his face with the sleeve of his shirt. "Damn, Mac will be turning over in his grave about now." He hobbled to his horse and mounted. "Let's get down the road, Quinn. I ain't doin' anybody any good here." Whistling a shrill note, he circled the horses they had. Shep led the way.

Quinn rode behind, rousting any strays or laggards. "Get up there, boys, that's it. Wheeew. Slow and easy." They stopped as the sun ducked behind the mountains with an eerie orange-red glow before snuffing out. They built a rope corral strung between the cedars, giving the horses an area of free movement. Quinn unpacked and began a fire for cooking while Shep attended the horses.

Both men were quiet, lost in their own thoughts. A coffeepot sat beside the fire, keeping warm. Their dirty plates leaned on rocks, not yet washed. A few biscuits had been placed in a bandana for breakfast in the morning.

Neither had spoken much during the drive. They made ten miles that first day, riding hard and fast to separate themselves from Trapper's men.

An uncomfortable time passed. Doves cooed their good night. Frogs called for mates. Darkness descended like a cool shadow.

"Don't know much about you, Quinn, 'cept what Jonny has said. How'd you two meet up?" Shepherd leaned against an old juniper log. He had taken off his boots and was warming his feet close to the fire.

"Funny you should ask that question. It was last winter, 1851. We was both on a train headed for Terre Haute, from Indianapolis. Colder than the devil. We were all sitting close to the only stove on the train. I was heading west for a train leaving Independence in the Spring.

"This boy was moving down the aisle to his seat, when the train lurched and this impertinent young man fell into my lap. He had a death grip on an old valise, so he couldn't brace himself. I told him to watch where he was going or I'd box his ears. I didn't like town boys very much. I had lived on the trail most of my life."

Shepherd broke a thin smile at the remembrance. "Jon probably looked like a baby to you then. He always had a face that looked younger than he was. Grew up fighting the bigger boys. We was raised on a horse ranch, and there wasn't a speck of fat on him. Wire thin, but stout as hickory. He won his fair share of the fighting and they learned to leave him alone." He threw a stick into the fire.

Quinn nodded. "Like I said, it was cold and the wind swept through that car as if there were no walls at all, but a young woman complained she was too close to the stove and moved farther back of the car as the heat was singeing her dress. I might add, she was quite attractive. Jon sat in a seat farther down the aisle from me. My buffalo coat kept me warm. I recall, I was reading a book called *Ben Hur*."

Shepherd looked at him with a disbelieving face. "You

read?"

Quinn shot him an offended glance. "Yes, I read. Like I said, I was reading, when three ruffians began accosting this woman I mentioned. She started screaming for help. Before, I knew it, I was in a fight for the lady's honor. It felt good to be active again. City living had dulled my wits, and I was mighty ready to getting back on the trail. I pushed the first one I came to toward the back of the train. 'You villains leave this lady alone,' I commanded. I try to sound like the heroes in my books when I am around women. They love it."

Shepherd rolled his eyes and chuckled. He felt a little envious.

"Well, it works for me." Quinn tilted his chin in pride. "The next thing I know, two of them had grabbed me, and the third was using me for a punching bag."

"Where's Jon in all of this?"

"I'm getting there. Like I said, I was holding my own with these assailants."

"You mean you were getting your arse kicked." Shep chuckled.

"Kinda sorta like that. When young Jonny boy came a calling, he pulled off the one using his fists on me. Punched the guy in the face and laid into him like a cyclone. He kicked one of the men in the stomach, making him lose his grip on me. It was a beautiful thing to behold. Between the two of us, we drove them off. I sent the last one flying out the door after a kick to the seat of his backsides. I remember the red-faced conductor chasing after them, shouting for them to stop.

"The lady thanked us for stopping her accosters, but when I tried to sit next to her, she shooed me away. You know, shoo, shoo. She used her hands like women do when they are trying to get rid of bugs or chickens or children." Quinn stared into the fire, getting lost in the past.

Quinn tipped his hat to the woman and turned away, bumping into Jonny, who sported a bruised lip. "Quinn Taylor." He offered his hand. "Appreciate your help, though I was doing pretty well myself."

"You were getting your arse kicked. It looked like to me, from where I sat," Jon said.

"See, I knew it." Shep laughed behind his hand. Quinn winced, then continued.

"Did it look that way to you? I felt I had them where I wanted them," Quinn told him in return. They both broke out in laughter. "You were right, young man. I was getting the worst of it. Again, my thanks." He rubbed his jaw then offered his hand again. This time, we did shake.

"Jonny McKinzey at your service. Late of Indianapolis. Soon to be headed to Independence and then to the western mountains of Oregon. If I can be of any further service, just whistle."

Jon slid into his seat, and Quinn joined him. "Wait a minute, mister. Not so close. We just met ya know." Jon placed his valise at his side away from Quinn.

"What? Oh, I'm sorry. I didn't mean to offend," Quinn told him. "I was interested in what you said. You're headed to Oregon? Me, too. Let me introduce myself properly. I am Quinn Taylor, head scout for The Hollyfield wagon train heading west to Oregon. We expect over one hundred wagons. Do you have anyone with you?"

Jonny shook his head.

"You're going to Oregon by yourself?"

"What of it?" he shot back. "I can take care of myself. As you can see. I pulled your fat out of the fire."

"Yes, you did. That's why I'm interested."

Jon's eyes narrowed. "What do you mean?"

"I need good men. You can handle yourself and think on your feet. Do you know how to drive a wagon and anything about horses. You seem pretty young."

Jon snorted. "Don't let my face fool you, Mr. Quinn. I

been breaking horses since I was ten. I've black smithed and pounded iron rims on wagon wheels for as long. I can make an anvil sing if I want."

"How about a job?" Quinn knew this was the kind of man he was looking for.

"What do you mean?" Jonny was wary, he had just met Quinn—who didn't act or talk like any wagon scout he had ever seen.

"I need teamsters for the train. I'm scouting for men who can ride and handle themselves all day long, if need be, without crying to their mama if their backsides gets sore."

Jon just smirked at Quinn, who'd dressed in town clothes. Fancy shirt and pants, shiny boots. He had worn his French perfume as well.

Realizing he wasn't coming across like much of a seasoned scout, Quinn tried to explain. "I'm the best scout you ever did see. I dress like this in town for the ladies. They don't want some dirty roustabout to buy them supper. I'll teach you what you need to stay alive out there on the big lonely." When Jon didn't comment, he pressed on. "Pay is thirty a month. We furnish blankets, mounts, and vittles. Can you use a gun and a rifle? What do ya say?"

"I don't know... I can carry my own water with a handgun. I'm better with a rifle."

Quinn could tell he was winning him over. "It would be nice to have a pocketful of money when you get to Oregon, wouldn't it?"

"I got money."

"Well, son, if your family fortune is in that valise you're hiding from me, you'll be safer as a teamster with a wagon to keep it in rather than a hidden saddlebag around a lot of people you don't know."

Jonny's face turned red. Quinn was on to his secret.

"Don't be a dolt, kid. I'm not interested in your money, but I can help you keep it and put more in your pocket at

the end of the trail."
Jon stared him straight in the eye. "Well alright."

Quinn returned to the present. He glanced at Shepherd. "It was the start of a long friendship.

Shepherd lit a smoke then exhaled, blowing the white smoke out against the black night. Wisps of fire sent sparks floating up the shaft of heat to burn out completely then disappear. "So, we have you to thank for Jon's safety on the trail west?"

"So to speak, I guess." Quinn sipped at his cold coffee. "I taught him how to stay alive. What to look for when the Injuns are setting to jump you. How to find water when there isn't any. Shot a snake once and made him eat it so he'd learn that you'll eat anything when you're starving. Your pa made a real man out of him. I just helped fine-tune the man he was."

"Pa would be real proud to hear that. I can hear it in Jon's voice. He isn't the boy we left behind to finish school. He is his own man."

"He's pulled my bacon out of the fire more than once. Picked me off the ground during a buffalo stampede when my horse fell and broke his neck. I still miss that horse. One of the best I ever rode. He and I held off a dozen braves once. We was down in a buffalo waller when they came at us. Killed three of them before they ran off. Our Colts were a surprise to them. We shot faster than they could re-load. So many mishaps on the trail, I can't recount them all, but we always watched out for each other. Jon was and is stout. I don't envy the men he is after. He'll track them down or die trying."

"You're right. Jon is steadfast. He does what he says he'll do."

"A good man to ride the river with, I've heard the old ones say. I'm proud he is my friend. I am only sorry that he had to come to his new home, to all of this…this tragedy."

Shep kept his thoughts to himself as he evaluated Quinn. "Jonny says you're going into the ranching business with us. Is that what you want to do?"

"I thought I might give it a try. I've lived on the trail most of life." Quinn shot him a halfhearted smile, as if he wasn't sure of his own statement.

"Never thought to ask you about your family. What happened to them?"

"Not much to tell." Quinn shrugged. "Indians killed my folks and my sister when I was about ten. We were headed to Kansas. Some hunters picked me up, buried my family, and took me under their care. An older man, Sir Robert Giel was his name, claimed he was from a wealthy family back in England, saw to me. Everybody called him Bob, much to his displeasure, but he accepted it once he realized it wasn't meant to denigrate his name. This lord took me under his wing. Why? Only he can answer that. Taught me to read and write. Gave me books and told me of wonderful stories of knights and Robin Hood, Ivanho. Did you ever learn of the Holy Crusades?"

Shepherd shook his head. "No. What's a Crusade?"

"I'll tell you one of these days. They were wonderful stories I've been reading ever since. Anyway, I grew up on the trail. Been on it ever since. I like to play the dandy in town. I was real shy around the ladies, but I learned to talk like Ivanho and the other heroes I read about, and they seemed to prefer my talk and dress over the hayseeds in town. Trouble was, I felt caged in town after a while. No woman wants a man who is always yearning to be off to parts unknown, not knowing if he's going to get an axe in his back."

"So, you're going to try ranching with us?"

"We'll see, Shep. We'll see." He tossed the remainder of his coffee into the fire. "I told Jonny I'd give it a try, but I'm not so certain I'm up to it."

CHAPTER 11

Jonny Mac fired at the moving shadow, hitting rocks. Bursting granite and lead fragments showered the face of the Indian creeping toward him. The shadow screamed and disappeared.

"I didn't get that one, but he'll be marked for sure."

Having Navy Colts was like owning hand cannons with six shots each. Jon quickly reloaded his Colt. He made sure all six chambers were loaded in both guns. They were marvels and the only way he had been able to keep the warriors at bay. With six shots for each cylinder and four cylinders, he had twenty-four cartridges before he had to reload. The Yoncallas had lost three men on their first charge into the box canyon after discovering Jon's hiding place. The last one wasn't dead, but he wouldn't be much use to anyone.

He and Derry made their way southwest, through the mountains. Gold City was somewhere on the Illinois River, south toward California. He planned to keep searching until he found it.

After a week of travel, the first Yoncalla had joined him on the trail, seemingly out of nowhere. He was friendly at first and signed for a smoke. Jon handed him the makings with no question. They rode silently for a while. The Indian noticed Jon's Colts and rode closer. He reached for a gun. Jon shied Derry away, speaking angrily at the Indian. "Keep your hands off that!"

Gesturing to Jon that he wanted a trade, the man stared at him intently.

Jon shook his head. "No." Derry sank his teeth into the offending pony's neck.

Fighting for control, the warrior reined up and disappeared back into the forest.

Forgetting about the Indian, Jon stopped on an overlook a few miles later to enjoy the view and to pick out the trail below as it hugged the mountainside. A loud clatter of hoofs on rock jolted him alert. The Yoncalla rode up alongside him with a young girl and three other horses trailing behind. Mud was smeared over his horse's neck. Emphatically signing, the Indian wanted to trade the horses and girl for Jon's guns.

"No." Jon signed and rode on.

Again, the Indian rode up bumping into Derry, demanding a trade. Derry lunged for the other horse, and the pair danced away frantically, fighting for control. He was a short lean man with a cape of beaten bark covering his shoulders. A beaten mat of bark folded over the top covered his greasy topknots of hair. His eyes were brown, and his round face was decorated with small cuts adorning his cheeks. Seashells hung from his neck, clicking each time he gestured. Jon sensed a pleading manner to his bargaining. The Colts would make him a big man in his tribe.

"No trade," Jon said louder and made a slicing move across his other palm. Done. Reining Derry back to the trail, he left the Indian scowling at his back.

Jon's guts began churning. Not a good sign. But if he ran, he would invite a chase, so he kept to the trail as if he were in no hurry, no danger. The Yoncalla followed at a distance.

He descended the trail, using the switchbacks, etched by thousands of years of animal instinct, carved into the mountain side. He glanced up to see if his shadow still followed. There were three of them. Hairs on the back of his neck stood up. His gut cramped a bit. Jon wiped the sweat from his face. It was hot and, from the looks of things, going to get hotter.

They were above a narrow valley, cut by other defiles from erosion and stream runoff. A waterfall gushing with bouncing waters over the round, smooth rocks came up on his left. He peered over his shoulder. A line of Indians descended, single filing down the narrow trail. He couldn't count them all because rocks and trees blocked his line of vision.

Now, his gut told him, was the time to make a run for it. Kicking Derry with his heels, they broke into a run, crow hopping and skidding down the length of the narrow snaky decline until they made it to the bottom. Jon gave Derry his head and bent low over him.

They flew like the wind. Derry moved as if his hoofs were wings. They ran full bore away from the rock face. By the time he could hear the whooping and shouts behind them, Jon's blood was up. The chase was on, and he and Derry were the foxes. This was the first time Jon had felt Derry's full power, so he let him have his head and Jon hung on.

Jon couldn't tell what was up ahead, so he kept the stream on his left for as long as he was able to, knowing it would flow out of these mountains eventually. They sprinted for a mile with the Indians never gaining on them.

The Yoncalla weren't going to catch Derry, but they could wear him down. The Indians knew these mountains, their ponies were bred to the steep valleys and lung-burning heights.

Suddenly, the stream cut in front of them, forcing Jon to

veer to the left, keeping the stream on his right. Another canyon opened to his left. Jon pulled up. Derry had plenty of go, but if he wore his horse down, all would be lost.

Turning back toward the stream, he rode for a little way. Seeing that the main canyon narrowed, he left the stream following the only trail through the mountain with steep walls on both sides. Jon backed up Derry and ducked into the off canyon they had seen earlier. The Indians weren't far behind. If his plan worked, the Indians would ride past them.

Hidden in the smaller canyon, Jon dismounted and hurriedly threw dirt and stones over their wet tracks, masking them from view then vanished deeper into the hidden canyon. The Indians' unshod mounts drummed the ground as they stormed past, shrieking and hollering, splashing into the stream and through the declivity of the slopes and out of view. Jon led Derry out and let him have a long drink. He filled his canteen and water bag then slipped back into the canyon. Finishing his subterfuge, he brushed out their tracks, hoping the Indians would continue their search farther down the canyon and not backtrack.

It was darker and cooler in the canyon. The sides of the steep terrain blocked out the sun this time of day. Derry's hooves clip-clopped on the stony floor, sounding like they were walking on broken china, echoing off the flint-sided defile. Jon dismounted, urging him closer to the opposite side where the ground was softer, not as loud. The floor of the canyon was thirty feet across, he guessed, and fifty to the top.

No trail leading up, only a faint line of sheep tracks led back into the unknown. Cool air wafted across his face as they rounded a shoulder of rock. A line of huge boulders blocked any further progress. Looking around, Jon discovered the sheep tracks following a dim narrow trail up the side of the rocks and going around behind the largest of the boulders. There he found an opening just big enough to squeeze through.

A small pool of water lay beyond and against the back wall of the box canyon, locking them in. Small rivulets of water dripped, feeding the pool. Water and a dozen knurled oaks and tufts of grass was what drew the sheep back into the canyon. A couple of acres or so he figured. Home for a while. He took the saddle from Derry and urged him through the opening. Using rocks and smaller boulders, he blocked the entrance as best he could while leaving an open firing slot. Nothing to do but wait. There would be no fire.

Jon tossed his saddle under some small oaks, pulled his hat over his eyes, and lay down. There might not be time for sleep later. Derry would let him know if anything came close.

He dared not leave the refuge of the canyon. No doubt, the Yoncalla had combed the hills looking for them. No fire, no coffee for Jon. Derry was fairly content. Much of the grass was chewed to the ground, so they could not stay here for more than a few days. Jon would not bear to see Derry starved again.

The third day, the Indians found them.

A scout brave had followed the sheep trail and knocked down the stones barring the small entrance. It was not his day to live. Jon shot him then rebuilt his wall. The shot brought the others. Changing position, Jonny Mac fired through the cracks between the boulders. Three Yoncallas died that day.

His position was good. If he kept moving, his enemies could not tell where he was firing from, but then realization set in. If the Indians somehow climbed the boulders and got on top of him, that would mean disaster. He would have to keep them at a distance. They knew where he was, so at least he could build a fire and make some coffee and soup.

The fourth day, they played games, trying to draw his fire and waste his ammunition. He fired one pistol until it clicked. Clicking it on the empty cylinder several more times drew the warriors out. Taking the bait, they charged, and Jon opened fire with his other gun bringing down two more. In the biting cordite and gun smoke, he changed cylinders. Just as quickly as they charged. A few Yoncallas shot in the air as a diversion while others came to drag their dead and wounded out of sight.

Jon reloaded his guns, watching out through cracks between the boulders. So far, it was a standoff. They couldn't burn him out. There was nothing to burn. Jon dozed, his face pressed to the coolness of the rock face.

Rain fell that evening, dampening the earth then built into a thunder and lightning storm with rolling clouds coming in from the sea. His slicker covering him, Jon sat underneath an overhang of rock, scrutinizing the crevices of the canyon before him. It stormed well past midnight before it subsided, leaving dripping freshets plopping fat drops into swollen puddles. Mist formed in the lower valleys as the moisture evaporated and the air cooled.

It was time to go. *Now or never.*

Jon quietly tore down his barrier, squatting to get through to the other side. He wanted to scout down the canyon to see if any guards had been posted, before bringing Derry out. He took off his slicker and boots, put on his moccasins then stole silently ahead to search the entrance of the canyon. Only one sentinel was found posted at the mouth of the canyon, asleep under his dirty sheepskin robe.

It looked like the Yoncallas had not come prepared for a long standoff. They were huddled under makeshift lean-tos, wrapped in sodden blankets. A smoky fire, trying to stay alive, illuminated the camp, casting long shadows and moving flickering lights, flitting from one place to another. The guard at the mouth of the canyon still dozed, his sheepskin covering him. His snores kept a rhythmic cadence, muffled in the dampness and mist. Echoes of the dripping wet rang off the rock face, sounding eerily sinister.

Jon returned and quietly saddled Derry. He wanted no metal jangles to wake the guard. He then cut pieces from his blanket and wrapped them around Derry's hooves to keep them quiet. Silently, they stole through the rocky stream bed, keeping to the sandy side. Moving through the mists, Jon planned to sneak past the guard and the sleeping warriors, into the stream, and around the bend of the stream, before he could mount and make his getaway without being noticed.

Jon led Derry toward the mouth of the canyon, reins in one hand, his Colt tucked beneath his belly in his belt. He hardly breathed. Suddenly, something reached out and touched his hand.

"Waa?" Jon stifled his response, automatically drawing his gun to bash whatever had touched him. "What are you doing here?" he hissed between clenched teeth.

It was the young girl the Yoncalla warrior had offered him. Her dress was torn and filthy, barely covering her. Looking wane and hungry, it was obvious, she had had little care from her captors. She put her finger to her mouth and indicated she wanted to go with him.

"I can't take you with me. Go back. Leave me alone." He grabbed her by her shoulders, turned her around, and gave her a shove toward the camp. Again, she indicated she wanted to go with him.

"You're going to get me killed, little girl." Jon's voice rose.

She put her finger to her lips then pointed to the guard who was now sitting up, trying to make out what was in the mist.

"Damn, damn, damn. Who was the guy who said to me to always make a plan? Now we've done it." Jon spit between his teeth before mounting Derry.

Looking down at the girl's pleading eyes, Jon gave in. "Oh, all right. No sense in only one of us getting killed."

He extended his hand and pulled her up behind him

Jon gripped a pistol in each hand and, squeezing onto Derry with both legs, let the reins lay loose over his saddle. "Hang on just as tight as you can, little lady. We're going fast."

The guard stood and moved a little toward them so he could see better.

"Here we go!" Jon whistled then put the reins in his mouth. "Hurrah!" His first shot was into the scrambling guard.

At full gallop, Derry burst out of the canyon mists like the fiery fiend that was his namesake. A Derrygonnally Fire Demon leaping the fire sent the Yoncallas' souls shaking at the sight, causing mad panic. Jon triggered both pistols, to the right and left, shooting into blankets, and dark standing and racing forms. Anything that moved. From horseback, he cut the string tethering the ponies, shooting and screaming his war cry into the air. Derry stomped and bit at the ponies, terrifying them into full flight up the valley floor.

The Yoncalla, who had wanted to trade, raced toward them, war club raised to bash in Jon's head. Jon shot him point-blank at the height of the man's leap. "There's some guns for you."

The misty wraith of fire horse-mounted evil raced down the canyon floor and into the stream, firing into any ill-fated pursuers fearless enough chase them.

That is how the story would be told around their campfires, back in the village.

Riding into the blackness of the night, they stayed in the stream until they were sure no one pursued. Jon stopped to remove the blanket wraps on Derry's feet.

"Phew! You stink, little lady." He helped her off Derry's back. "Here." He dug in his saddlebag and brought out a bar of soap and tossed it to her.

She held it, looking lost. Jon mimicked washing himself,

until she smiled in recognition. Then she pulled off her dress, jumped into the cold water, and began washing.

"Make it quick." He pulled out a shirt and hung it on a branch. "Put this on when you're finished. It's better than the rag you're wearing...or were wearing," he said, embarrassed at her unconcern for his presence. "What have I got myself into?"

He learned that her name was Aloosa. She kept pointing out which trails to take and would strike him in his chest when he ignored her and tried to take a trail she didn't want him to go on.

"Hey! That hurts."

"Cooos," she uttered happily, using her hand to wave over a wide area.

"Cooos," he repeated and waved over the land as she had before. He guessed these were lands she knew, perhaps her tribal lands.

Happily, she nodded and struck his chest with her fist then pointed to the trail on their right.

Her directions took him west of where he thought he should be going, but he gave in to her pointing fingers, more to keep from getting hit with her persuasive sharp fists than anything. He was heading west, and he hoped she was a safe guide.

That night, after a quick meal, Aloosa talked to him, gesturing about and pointing west and north of where they camped.

He hoped she was saying her tribe was friendly and not cannibalistic. Some tribes were. He had heard the diet on these coasts was mainly sheep, fish, and plants, but some still practiced eating human flesh for certain ceremonies. Aloosa chattered away by the fire, her knees drawn up under her, covered in a blanket, until she grew quiet and pensive, pondering her own thoughts. Exhausted, Jon fell into his blankets gratefully. Winds from the coast filtered through the grasses, blowing sand, releasing pine-scented perfume into the night air, crooning them to sleep.

Aloosa was gone in the morning. Jon wasn't surprised, and he made no effort to find her. She was familiar with the country. He guessed she was headed back to her tribe. After coffee and the last of his bacon, he turned Derry's nose to the south. By midmorning, they were on a sandy rise, looking at a trail bordering the Rouge River. A well-used trail led east. Gold City lay to the east somewhere on the Illinois. They took it.

Gold City was where the Nolans were. Jon formulated a plan as he traveled. His gut told him it was good to be alone again. He still had unfinished business.

CHAPTER 12

S heriff Lyle Newton glanced over the swinging doors into Kate Marston's café. She served good food and the best baked goods in town. He was on a mission. One he didn't enjoy. He spied his men back in the corner, reading newspapers and eating breakfast.

He pushed open the doors and stood in the doorway, eyeing them.

Shep shivered. "Here it comes, brother. The sheriff is walking our way."

Quinn immediately came to attention, catching the long form of the lawman as he stopped in front of them. He laid his paper on the table. "Shep, would you pass me the sugar. Mornin', Sheriff. Care for breakfast?" Quinn kicked a chair from underneath the table toward the standing form. He looked up at the expressionless face. "Nice day, isn't it?"

Shep picked up the sugar in one of his large hands and set it in front of Quinn then waited. Something was bothering Sheriff Lyle, and somehow, it involved him and Quinn.

"Thanks, boys." Lyle sat down. "I see you're up and about. Must feel good, not having to hobble around with a stick. Seen Jonny lately?"

Both men straightened. "Haven't seen him since before

we brought in our horses. Me and Quinn have been rebuilding the ranch. We don't come any farther than town, when we want some of Kate's pie. Kate makes very good pie."

"Yes, she does, Shep. The best." He settled into his chair then leaned forward so no one else could hear what he had to say. "Don't look at me with snake eyes, boys. I've been on Jonny's side all along. You know that. Trouble is…there is a warrant out for Jon, Jonny Mac, Jonny McKinzey's arrest. I gotta find a couple of fellas to go after him and bring him back for trial. They could get killed by Jonny. If that happened, he'd be a hunted man for the rest of his life."

Shep started to get up.

"Sit down, Shep," Lyle told him. "I've got it worked out. You see, I've found the two best men to go after Jonny McKinzey."

The air between the three men grew tense with unsaid expectations.

"What are the charges, Sheriff?" Quinn shifted in his chair. It wasn't comfortable anymore for some reason.

"So far, there have been seven charges of murder and accounts of property damage and horse thievin'."

"You saw the horses when we brought them back. You knowed they are our horses. All MCK brands, except the colt. We told you the story." Quinn drank some coffee then cut into the wedge of pie on his plate and forked some in his mouth. Chewing a piece of golden raisin and plum pie made him smile. "I don't see the problem."

"I don't, either, Sheriff." Shep studied Lyle's face.

"Here's the case that's being made against Jonny. He's outside the law. Oregon is trying to qualify for statehood. The governor wants these killings stopped and Jonny brought in for trial. Everybody is complaining. They want a trial so they appear to the U.S. government's review board that we are a law-abiding place to live. We're simply a territory right now. Big things happen when you get to statehood. Our governor is ambitious. I have the job of bringing him in."

"So why come to us?" Quinn looked at Shep.

"I know you two are going to go find him. Don't argue. It won't do any good. I know you fellas. You're going after him. That's why you been laying in supplies whilst you're in town. Shep, you can walk and ride. And, Quinn, you're so agitated, you acts like you got bugs in your pants." He leveled his gaze on each of them in turn. "If you love your brother, you'll help me."

"So, send these men you've chosen. Why tell us?" Shep returned to his paper.

"'Cause you're the men I've chosen." He sat back with a smug grimace on his face, arms across his chest.

Quinn appeared stunned. "You are crazy. Why would we go after Jonny. We're on his side."

"You've got something up your sleeve, don't ya? Well, I'm not going along with it. Get someone else." Shep challenged Sheriff Lyle with his stare.

"I know. I know. He's your brother and all. You think I'm not on your side, but I am. Listen." He motioned for them to come closer. "You know where Jon is headed. Any other men would have to search for months to find him. If he is killed or kills a lawman, he will never live as a free man ever again. He'll either die on the run or in some hellish prison somewhere, busting rocks till his back gives out and the warden lets him run away and guards kill him. Life in prison is nothing you want for Jonny. I don't, either."

"You say you got a plan?" Shep was a lot more intrigued.

Quinn leaned forward as well.

"I can make you both deputy marshals. I got the papers from the governor. Jonny won't shoot you. Bring him in. He'll go to trial. I'll do my best to have the governor throw it out."

"I still won't do it. Is there a sworn affidavit that Jonny will be set free?" Quinn pushed the table away and stood up.

"One more thing, Shepherd." Lyle held his arm. "The Exclusion Act excludes Negros from settling in Oregon. For any reason, they are being forced to leave, and it is sticking in court. If you become a deputy, you are subject to US government law and are outside Oregon territorial jurisdiction."

"Lyle, you've heard us to swear revenge on the gang that killed Pa. You know what we're going to do."

"Yes, I do, but I'll never swear to it. Gold City is in Indian territory. No law. Go find the Nolans. The Indians will like white men killing white men. White law overlooks whatever happens in Indian country. Bring Jon back to your ranch. I have contacts with the judges around here. I'll do my best to get him off. You're the only two men who can save Jonny McKinzey's life. You're the only ones." Lyle spread his arms wide. "There it is."

CHAPTER 13

—◈—

J on pulled the curtain back from the window in the Gold Spider Hotel, surveying the street for the Nolans. He had arrived two days earlier, scouting and watching activity in town, signing the register as J.M. Smith to avoid suspicion.

Gold City was a hell town. Main Street had seven saloons, two cafés, a Chinese laundry and opium den, and two hotels. All structures had been carelessly built next to each other, except for an occasional alleyway from the local pine forest. Women wantonly plied the oldest ruse in the world, under anything that would shed water. There were wagons, canvas tents, upstairs in the saloons, and in one of the cafés, busy night and day. Pigs wandered the alleyways that weren't occupied. A secluded run-down stable at the far end of the street was crowded with horses in its corrals. One could get rich, but at the same time, life was cheap.

For the last several days, as he moved through the streets of the town, Jon had observed men drinking, getting drunk, falling down then getting up to go drink some more. They visited brothel after brothel until they ran out of funds. After dusting themselves off, they washed their faces in cold water, drank pots of coffee, and returned to prospecting. Oftentimes, a gunfight arose over cards, whiskey, women, and or, horses. Bodies were left on the boardwalks until the undertaker had time to pick them up. Seven dead in one day was the record the city held. The town reminded Jon of Hieronymus Bosch paintings he had seen back in school.

This place disgusted him, but he knew what he had come for. He observed the Nolan's habits. Steve and Lucky visited the opium dens daily. Whitey held court at the Nugget saloon. They ate at the café next door. Jon made his plans, and he was ready to instrument them.

He needed to visit the Chinese laundry to learn the layout. Walking by the café, he glanced in the window. No Nolans about. The name of the laundry in rusty red paint had been written in Chinese and English, Wash Clothes/Pleasant Dreams. The bell affixed to the door startled him as he entered.

Lucky and Steve Nolan had visited the den two nights in a row. He was betting they would continue their routine. He would visit the Nugget after his surveillance of the place of dreams and clean clothes.

Never having been in an opium den, Jon wanted to see what it was like. The attendant asked him in Chinese; then, seeing no recognition, he asked in English. "You like have happy smoke?"

Jon nodded. He was escorted through a closed door. They passed by stacked beds with curtains overhanging for privacy. Smoke and soft coughing lingered in the air. When his escort wasn't watching, Jon snatched a curtain back, revealing a prone body peacefully snoring, the cold pipe still between his teeth. "So, this is what they do here."

The pungent sweet musk wafting in the air was enticing. Jon refused the offer of a pipe, a candle, and a ball of tar-like consistency with profound apologies to his escort, who pursed his lips and swore in Chinese at him.

Jon held up his hands in surrender and quickly retraced

his steps, leaving the same way he had come in.

When he spied two men crossing the street, alarm rose up his back. *Lucky and Steve!* He pretended to trip, using his hand to cover his face as the two men passed him on the sidewalk, heading toward the laundry. After the close call, he realized they had no idea who he was or what he looked like.

Jon noted the time on his watch, eight thirty. He had observed them without arousing suspicion or being seen, and this was the third night in a row they had visited the opium dens. Their routine had become clear. After waking up, they went to the café at about noon, then they returned that night for another go-round at the den.

Jon next visited the Nugget saloon. After buying a beer, he sidled over to the end of the bar to stand in the partial shadows. The dim light and cigar smoke made it difficult for him to search for Whitey. A brightly painted woman sang on a stage with a chorus of four women tossing their skirts and dancing around her. Men shouted at each other. Men bet on faro and roulette, spilling gold dust from leather pouches as they pressed to the tables in their excitement of a quick strike.

He spoke to the bartender when a dripping glass of beer was set in front of him. "I'm looking for Whitey Nolan. We got a horse deal to see about. When does he come in?"

The bartender scowled. "Who are you, son? You don't look old enough to savvy any of Whitey Nolan's tricks."

Jon smiled. "I'm sitting in on this due to my daddy, Trapper Jack, couldn't make it. When does this Whitey come in?" He sipped his beer, watching the bartender's eyes.

"He don't come in till after ten o'clock, mos' ususallies." He glanced at a table of men off in the far corner. "How's the beer?"

"Not bad. Colder than what I expected. Thanks." Jon kept to himself.

He followed the bartender in the mirror. When the man slid through the crowd over to a table back in the smoke-filled room, Jon melted into the shadows, slipping away before anyone at the table could turn his way. From a darkened doorway under the balcony, he could see the bartender pointing his way then searching for him while trying to explain to someone at the table Trapper Jack's kid had just asked for him.

On the street, Jon stepped into the narrow alley between buildings, waiting for Whitey to come out, searching for Trapper Jack's kid. Whitey exited the Nugget saloon doors, peering up and down the street with a quizzical expression on his face then going back inside.

Jon noted the time. "One hour should do it."

Jon arrived at the laundry at eight o'clock the next evening. He carried a rope and wore both guns holstered. The attendant was dismayed to see him, but Jon begged forgiveness and asked for a pipe. All was forgiven immediately. The attendant clapped his hands twice, and a young girl appeared with a lit lamp, pipe, and tarry opium egg. They were led to a bed, and the attendant opened the curtain. Jon waved him off, indicating he wanted to go deeper into the room to a bed in the back. The attendant appeared surprised before he turned and led him to where he wanted to go. This was where the frequent guests came to dream their fears and wishes away.

Both he and the young girl were shown to the bottom bed of the three-bed stack. Jon checked for anyone down the corridor, before he and the girl disappeared behind the dark curtains. The girl offered him a loaded pipe and tried to light it for him. He pushed her back into the bed. After blowing out the lit wick, he put his fingers to his lips then to hers.

"Shhh." He used his arms and hands to indicate to her everything was all right, then he shushed her again.

She nodded in understanding.

Steve and Lucky's laughter echoed from the front room. Jon could not understand what they said as they walked down the corridor. They were settled on respective beds, Steve on a top bunk, and Lucky had the bed next to Jon but on the middle level. Pipes were lit, and the girls exited the room. Steve and Lucky lay down into dreamland. Jon pushed his girl out, too, urging her to follow the others.

All was still as he waited. Soft snores sounded with occasional cries of pleasure. No one was about, all was ghostlike, a living, smoke-induced, dream morgue. Jon crept out of his bed.

He tugged at Lucky's curtain. Lucky mumbled in his sleep. Jon nudged him harder.

Lucky sat up. "Eh. What?"

"Hello, Lucky." Jon held up a bowie knife. He let the golden shine of the lanterns gleam on the blade's surface for Lucky's eyes to feast on.

Lucky shook his head trying to clear it briefly. "Hello?"

"Remember the McKinzey's, Lucky? How about my pa, Lucky? Do you remember Mac McKinzey?"

"McKinzey?" Lucky's eyes opened wide in realization. "Noo!"

Jon cut Lucky's throat in one deep slashing sweep. He used the curtain to hold him down and stifle the death groan. It was over in a few moments. No one had been alarmed. When he finished, Jon wiped the blade on Lucky's pillow.

"Hey, Lucky? You say something?" Steve's hand fell off the bed and hung there, not moving.

"Okay, Steve," Jon softly croaked, hoping the man would assume it was Lucky.

Soft snores returned to Steve's bed. Jon retrieved the rope.

Voices from down the corridor alerted him. Jon crept back into his bed. He lit his pipe and let the smoke drift into his chamber. When the attendant opened the curtain, Jon pretended to be unconscious, a smoldering pipe still in his lips. The attendant pulled closed the curtain and admonished the young girl as he forced her to go back to the front of the house.

Jon crept over to Steve's bunk and nudged him with his gun barrel. Steve did not flinch. Moving quickly, he tied Steve's feet securely to the end of the bed, then he tied the brother's hands behind his back. Gently, Jon slipped a noose over the sleeping man's neck and snugged it. So far, no one made a noise or took notice of Jon's movements. After he was finished, he slapped Steve's face until he woke up, cross-eyed and befuddled.

"Hello, Steve." Jon held a lamp up to his face, so Steve could see him.

"Er, who are you?" Steve blinked a blank face, struggling to open his eyes.

"I am the revenge of the McKinzeys. Remember them?"

Terror started at the base of Steve's neck then crossed into his face. He sat straight up. "McKinzey!"

Then Jon dragged him out of the bed.

Steve fell about two feet before the noose around his neck caught him short. His feet were tightly bound to the foot of the bunk. He had no support for himself. All of his weight was on his neck. Jon yanked the noose tighter. "Remember what you did to my brother's folks back in Indiana? This is what it feels like to hang."

Steve rolled and twisted in his struggles, gurgles rose in his throat, but the rope cut deeper and deeper until he gagged on his last breath and his movement stopped. Jon pulled his bowie to finish what he had started.

Finished with the job, Jon stumbled out of the drug house of death, waving that he was all right to the attendant. Glad to be in the fresh air, he took a deep gulp of air, hoping to clear his head. Straightening up, he walked down to the Nugget, creeping into the shadows as before. Whitey was playing cards with four other men at the table from earlier. An older man with a shotgun sat behind Whitey, like he was guarding the game.

"Here ya go, Winfro. See if those deuces you got showing will do you any good." A wide grin across his face, Whitey dealt around the table. "First ace bets. Go ahead, Shoshone Bill. What do you want?"

Bill tapped the table with two fingers. He checked.

So that's Winfro, and that old guy with the shotgun must be the last of the gang. All three of them, right here. Jon moved closer to the table of men.

A Chinese girl ran into the saloon, screaming for Whitey in broken English. "All gone. All brothers all gone!"

"What brothers? What is she saying? Can anybody tell me what she is saying?" Whitey looked about the room.

"All brothers. Dead. Dead. White man make dead. Not Chinese man. White man make dead." She pointed toward the laundry.

The male attendant burst through the batwing doors and went straight to Whitey. He whispered in his ear.

"What? That's impossible, hung?" Whitey stood, his face blanched by the news.

The attendant whispered in his ear again, making marks in the air with his fingers.

"MCK? They had McKinzey's brand carved into their chests?"

The attendant nodded with great vigor. "White man kill them. Not Chinese."

"Mind if I sit in?" Jon slipped into the vacant chair at the table. He held one of his Colts across his lap.

Whitey looked at him. "Who the hell are you?"

Winfro pushed back his chair, standing up with his hand on his gun. "No one sits here unless invited."

"You Winfro?"

"Yeah, I am."

"I'm Jonny McKinzey." He shot Winfro in the chest, knocking him back into the old man.

Whitey immediately drew and fired. Jon fired back. Both shots went wide in the excitement. A shotgun blast ripped the air past Jon's head. He bent and threw his chair at the old man then bolted for the door. He was no match for a shotgun. Not up this close. Better to retreat and fight in more open surroundings.

Running down the boardwalk, he found the way blocked by a crowd from the laundry turning out to see what the gunfire was about. Some carried lit torches. They tried to stop him, but he pushed his way through the crowd by waving his pistol at them. "Out of my way!"

One of the torch carriers tripped as Jon ran past, falling through the door. The house of paper and sticks caught fire and burst into flame. The crowd tore off their jackets and coats in an effort to beat down the fire.

The confusion slowed Whitey and his men as they exited the saloon, looking for Jon.

"I see him," Whitey yelled. "He's headed down the street."

Jon ran like the Yoncallas were after him, toward the stable at the end of town.

Whitey chased after him, firing wildly.

Behind Jon, shouts for help echoed against the fiery building.

"Help! Man the water brigade! The town is burning."

Whitey's friends dropped away to man the buckets. It was their town and their businesses. Whitey could fight his own battles.

Jon closed the doors to the stables then climbed the ladder into the loft, settling behind stacks of hay bales. A soft creaking from below told him Whitey was pushing the doors open. Bright orange and red shadows of the fire reflected off the stable walls. Smoke wafted in from the burning buildings.

Whitey crept into the barn. No one spoke. They didn't have to. Each was hunting the other.

Sliding down a rope, Jon landed behind Whitey. "Right here, Whitey."

Whitey turned, firing at shadows. Jon shot him.

Smoke filled the barn from the rapidly burning town.

"Damn you, McKinzey."

Stepping through the smoke, Jon smashed him in the face with his gun butt.

Whitey fired a round as he fell to the ground, grazing Jon across his right hip.

Staggering to stay on his feet, Jon grabbed at the wound and struggled to hold on to his pistol.

With a cry of desperation, Whitey tried to tackle him, but Jon shot him, hitting his shoulder. Whitey fell back onto the floor, dropping his gun, his right arm useless.

"What else you got, kid? I'm finished." Whitey's face was ashen, but his voice was defiant. "I got Mac McKinzey. That's all I care about."

"I know. I got all the Nolans tonight. That's all I've cared about since I got here." He reloaded his gun. "You're not done yet, Whitey. Not for what you done to Pa and Shepherd. Get up!" He kicked him in the ribs. "Get up!"

Whitey used his good arm to pull himself up a post to standing. Jon pushed him toward the corral.

"Where we going?" The man stumbled, catching himself at the door.

Jon used his foot to shove him into the corral's dirt. The horses scampered over to the far end of the enclosure. Whitey tried to stand.

Jon shot him in the knee. "Stay there."

Whitey screamed, crumpling to the ground.

"Watch for it, Whitey. Here they come." Jon shot into the air, moving the horses in a circle. "This is for you, Mac."

Panicked, Whitey tried to crawl away from the slashing legs and hooves. At first, they avoided his prone figure. Jon ran them faster and faster with each shot. Their circle tightened, fear gripping the herd of horses, until they trampled over Whitey with shodden hoofs, cutting him to ribbons. Jon kept shooting until he was out of bullets.

It was over.

"There he is! Where's Whitey? I tol' ya that McKinzey had him."

A shotgun blast caught Jon in the back and across his buttocks and leg. Grimacing, he dropped to the ground, crawling over to the water trough, pushing himself with one good left leg.

Horses still ran in circles in the corral. "Oh my God. That's Whitey! He's all smashed to pieces."

Another shotgun blast peppered the trough and ground in front of Jonny. The old man ran forward with cartridges in his hand. He broke the shotgun and started loading.

Jon shot him with his backup Colt. The old man fell forward, spilling the cartridges on the ground, and landed face down in the dust and horse droppings.

Jon pulled himself up, using the trough as a support. The horses milled on the far side of the corral. What was left of Whitey Nolan was a sodden shirt and hat trampled into the bloody mud. Jon struggled to climb the fence rail, but the heat from the inferno blasted his face. Holding a hand up for a shield, he viewed the burning town. The stable hadn't caught fire yet, but sparks flew through the air.

His back burned like a living hell. Gritting his teeth with determination, he climbed the corral fence. Through pursed and parched lips, Jon whistled for Derry. The horse appeared, a wraith emerging from the smoke, and sidled up to him. Jon fell from the top rail onto his saddle.

"Got 'em, Derry. Got every last one of them." He collapsed over the horse's neck. "Go."

They vanished into the blackness of the night,

swallowed up by the flickering shadows cast by the burning town.

Bucket brigades were abandoned. People fled for their lives. The blistering inferno devoured the town, casting vivid reds and oranges. Large pine trees blazed like torches, exploding into flame, one after another.

CHAPTER 14

Quinn rode up to Shepherd. They had been camped on the crest of the hill overlooking the Illinois River. Shepherd had broke camp and was mounting his horse.

"They told me Jon left there three nights ago," Quinn reported. "Five men were left dead in the dirt, including every last Nolan. The town burned to the ground. Not enough of Whitey was left to bury. He was trampled to death in the corral. Ain't nothing left of the whole town, 'cept the stable, soot, and ashes. Couldn't even recover or identify the bodies from the fire."

"What'll we do now? He could have gone anywhere." Shepherd stood up in his stirrups, surveying the forests. "You traveled with Jon. You know him better than me at this time in his life. Where would he go if you was him?"

"He was shot up and bleeding, hanging on to his horse for dear life as he rode away. Several of the Chinese saw him. Shep, if I was him, shot up as he is, I would want to hide somewhere. My guess, he's headed for the Shoshone camp. He has friends there, outside the law."

"I can't help but wonder what is happening to the boy I remember. He has turned into a man to ride the river," Shepherd said. "All this killing. It is breaking my heart to know what this must be doing to him. Thank God, that chapter is finally over. Did ya see any sign of Jonny at all?"

"There's only one trail leading north from the stable. Let's follow it and see if we can find any trace of them."

Shep waved him on. "Lead the way. You're a better tracker than me."

A few miles out, Quinn dismounted to examine the track in the trail. "Only one horse has come this way for several days. Too much sand to say for sure, but it must be Derry's tracks. They're going slow, not running, didn't see any blood, but in this sand, I may have missed it. Here, it cuts back into the mountains going east."

Shepherd followed the trail through the trees where Quinn had pointed. He examined the foliage on the trees as he rode. "Here ya go. Blood." Shepherd held up a leaf for Quinn to see. "That's dried blood if I ever did see it. We're on the right trail."

"He's got a big start on us. Maybe holed up somewheres or passed out or dead, for all we know. Derry could go all night if need be. They could be anywhere in those mountains east of us. Too many questions we don't know the answer to. Follow me." Quinn brushed by Shepherd, keeping his eyes and ears alert for anything that might happen. Lots of danger lurked in these mountains.

He cut a chaw, ruminating on the mountains looming around them. "Lots of ups and downs in those mountains. Trails twisting and turning. You could ride for an hour and still not be more'n three or four miles from where you started. All we can do is try for it. My daddy used to tell me, 'You have to start first to begin anything.'"

Quinn kicked his horse and took up the chase, Shepherd riding close behind him. Neither knew if Jon was alive or dead.

◆◈◆

Derry looked back at Jon who hadn't moved in an hour, ever since he had fallen out of his saddle with a loud thud and muttered groan. Derry drank from the stream, grazed, and had tried to throw his saddle off. He was bored and a bit curious. The smell of blood was strong with his friend, but it smelled old, not as fresh as it used to.

Nudging Jon with his nose hadn't done any good earlier. He tried again.

Jon groaned. That was better.

He nudged him again.

Jon cried out, startling Derry, by jumping away.

Determined now, Derry returned, nudging him harder. This brought a flutter to Jon's eyes, and he lay there looking up at the sky in utter incomprehension. Derry's soft nose nuzzled Jon's face, and Jon turned with a question in his eyes.

"Derry? Is that you? I thought I had died. I was dreaming of Ma and Pa. They were holding my firstborn child...my baby... Where am I?" Jon pushed himself up to his elbows, catching himself, wincing with stiffness and pain. "Derry, you did it, getting us away from there, but where is here?" His voice was so weak it cracked.

The sounds of a stream trickling over stones reached his ears, coming somewhere just past where Derry stood. He rolled over and onto his knees, but his head swam, and he thought he was going to be sick. He toppled onto his back.

Slowly, painfully, he crawled to the stream and drank. "Ah, that is better." He lay himself into the cold water, letting it flush pain and irritation away, until his head went under. "Shoot, waaa," he sputtered and spit water out of his mouth and nose.

He yelped taking his shirt off, the stuck scabbing blood pulling at his wounds. *I can't tell how many pellets are lodged in my back.* Even the superficial wounds brought wincing pain as sharp as the deep ones. His right hip was the worst. He couldn't move it without excruciating pain, but it would move. Altogether, he felt like a living piece of raw meat.

He crawled to Derry and, using his stirrup, pulled himself to standing. He dug around in his saddlebags until he found a clean shirt and tugged it over his head.

"All right, Derry, you've been doing pretty good. No one is following us. Just take it easy and slow. These fevers are making my head spin." It took three tries before he was able to mount.

"Let's go, Derry." He pointed the stallion up the creek. With no idea where they were, he set out, heading north and east.

The flush of fever washed up his body, like tiny prickles standing each hair straight up, starting in his legs and then washing up his back to his head, partially blinding his vision, leaving him disorientated and woozy.

"It's okay, Pa. I'm going to see Ma soon. I hope she has some biscuits. I miss her biscuits." Grasping Derry's mane, he held on until the heated rush passed.

Shaking his head to clear his eyes, Jon grimly rode on. He wasn't certain how bad he was wounded, but he needed help to get the lead out of his back. If not, the spreading poison in his body would eventually kill him. He had seen men die of such infections on the wagon train. He swore under his breath, determined to continue. He must find the Shoshone.

"Easy, Derry. Keep it slow." Riding cautiously through the forest, the fever again flushed his body, torturing his back, flooding his face with sweat and nausea. Every bump and jolt punished him. Stopping often to drink or bathe his back in a stream was all he could do. He was wobbly in the saddle after a few hours and his vision blurred. Jon pulled off his shirt, wet it in a stream, and draped it across his shoulders. There was bleeding when he turned too sharply, and he could feel tiny rivulets of blood and pus oozing down his back and leg into his trousers.

Slumping over Derry's neck, he fell into delirium. "This one is for Pa, Whitey. Take that!" He dreamed of the men he had killed menacing him, screaming at him while hideous tortures of hell consumed their bodies, but they never perished. "No, no, not that! Go away. Go away."

He shook himself. "Aawww!" He screamed himself awake from the dreams after falling into some horrible pit of doom, chased by monsters and devils, until he fell back into his body with a thud which woke him, nearly throwing him out of the saddle. "Uuugh!"

Sweat covered his face and dripped from his chin onto Derry's neck. That evening, sick and delirious, it took every bit of strength he had to stay in the saddle.

Jon shivered. His clothes were wet from perspiration. An evening breeze crept through the forest, chilling him to his core. His face flashed with heat, his body trembled, but he couldn't get himself warm. He looked out through squinted eyes, trying to make some sense of where he was, but nothing made any impression on his fevered mind. Shapes in the forest beckoned to him.

"Derry, did you see that? What was it?" He tried to see deeper into the woods.

Small animals appeared, weaving in through the trees chased by the demons from his dreams.

"No, nooo!"

Animals flying off through the trees and up into the sky, coming back to swoop down on him. He waved his arms in the air.

"Get away. Get away." Jon leaped off Derry in fright and started running, looking back in terror at charging demons. "Nooo! Run, Derry. Get away."

Flailing his arms over his head, he ran, but his body could not sustain him for long. He stumbled through the forest, imagining devils and spirits chasing him. Blinded by sweat and fear, he plowed into a huge-trunked pine, blacking out from the impact and delirium. He collapsed in a heap on a thick bed of pine needles, muttering protests and flapping his hands in the air.

Derry followed and nickered, but Jon did not get up.

CHAPTER 15

"Looks like he got off his horse over here. Here's pieces of his shirt. It's torn up somthin' awful. Full of blood, too. He must be hurt purty bad, Shepherd."

"That's how it looks to me, too, Quinn. Derry must be doing the thinking. He's going into places a man would stay out of. At least he's leaving a good track that's easy to follow. Let's keep going. He shouldn't be much farther ahead at the pace they're going."

The two men continued tracking their quarry. They headed northeast, following creeks and cuts through the mountains, going deeper and deeper into the forest. Later that afternoon, they came upon a game trail with clear hoofprints leading into a meadow with a small clear lake. Derry stood at the edge of the forest next to a grandpa pine tree. Jon lay stretched out on his stomach when they found him.

"Well, looka here, Shep. Somebody has done been doctoring him. They got some kinda poultice on his wounds." Quinn lifted an abalone shell, lying next to Jon, smelling it.

Quinn examined Jon's back. "Hmmm, this looks like mud, charcoal, and moss. Crude but fairly effective. Used a poultice on snakebites like this, once before. I wonder who did this." He looked around the forest's edge. A rustle of leaves caught his attention off to his right, but he could not make out anyone.

A few birds flew up a little farther on, but it only deepened the mystery in his mind. "Hey, hey! Come back." Quinn stood in silence, bowl in hand.

"Look, Quinn, you see what you can do fer Jon there. I'll see to Derry and set up a lean-to over by that lake there. Where do you want to put him?"

"Help me get him under some cover. He is still burning up from fever. I'm going to clean these wounds and see what needs to be done. That buckshot has got to come out. Set up the lean-to first. I don't want to move him again once I cut them out. We're going to have to keep him on his stomach. Let's get to it."

Shepherd set up the lean-to quickly and heated water over a fire so Quinn could wash Jon's wounds. They carried Jonny over to the lean-to and tried to make him as comfortable as they could lying on his stomach. Their patient did not move or make a sound.

Quinn stripped off the tattered clothes, surveying the damage. "Looks like whoever shot him shot too low. Jon only got part of the blast across his back and buttocks. He must have had a painful ride to this place. Whoever put on these poultices did a good job. It has started drawing the poison out of his wounds, which are mortifying. I got to get that lead out before the infection gets into his blood. Bring me a pan of hot water, will you, Shep, I intend to clean these holes. I count three holes across his back and two in his back sides. There's a graze burn on his hip. Not from a shotgun. Looks like they skimmed across his back, ripping the flesh and burying into the top layer of muscle."

"I'm heatin' up my skinning knife for ya, Quinn. I got it sharper than a madwoman's tongue."

"I'm going to need a sharp knife, that's for sure." He

fingered the blade. "I could skin a buck with this."

Shepherd moved to help. "What do you want me to do?"

"Hold him down as much as possible. Sit on him if you have to. This is going to hurt like hell. I don't know how long he will be unconscious. I could cut him bad if he twitches when I'm digging out a ball. This will be tricky. You got any of that whiskey left? We're all going to need a pull on that when this is over. Hurry up. We're losing light."

Shepherd looked at his friend with worry on his mind. He had prepared as best he knew how. They had clean moss. The abalone shell of pine pitch and moss they found laid on the ground next to Jon, warmed by the fire. These would help the wound heal, he hoped, and draw out any infection, if the infection was surface deep, as it looked.

Taking a deep breath, Quinn bowed his head in a brief prayer.

"It's all right, Quinn." Shep placed his hand on his shoulder. "You ever done this before?"

Quinn nodded. "Yeah, I cut some lead out of a few pilgrims coming over the Rockies, shot up by renegades. One of them died in my arms. Fixed a woman's broken leg once. She finished the trail walking on both of her legs."

"You can do it. You know you can. Take a deep breath. Take your time. Your experience will do the rest."

Quinn used a willow twig to probe the first shot wound closest to him. Jon moaned and tried to pull away from the source of the pain. "Hold him down, Shep. I'm going to be okay. Here we go."

Quinn made his first cut. He used his fingers to pinch the ball out which rolled across Jon's back and fell to the ground.

He smiled at Shepherd. "First one. That was easier than I thought it would be." Using bits of moss dipped in the poultice mixture, Quinn pushed it into the small hole to staunch the bleeding. He removed lead from the more superficial wounds first, letting himself get the feel for what he was doing, building confidence with each ball he rolled out of Jon's back and onto the ground. Some of the wounds had a fragment of a ball, but most were complete. The two deepest, he left until last.

"Want a drink of whiskey, Quinn? I sure could use one, and you've earned a drink. That's for sure."

"I'll get one when I'm finished. Please, lay across his back. He's coming around and I need to finish this before he wakes up."

The ball closest to the middle of his back was what Quinn concentrated on next, hoping nothing was broken this close to the spine. There was little he could do for a broken vertebra. Inserting the probe into the hole in Jon's back, he felt the roundness of the ball. Jon screamed and thrashed around, out of his head.

Shep pushed him down and wrapped his arms around Jon's arms, pinning them into the blankets. "Get it out, Quinn. He's almighty strong."

Quinn pinched the ball between his fingers, holding it steady then sliced down until he felt the lead under his blade and sliced across the ball, making room to excise it. He squeezed, exploding the ball to the surface, followed by blood, pus, and gore that spurted out of Jon's back and across Quinn's shirt.

The smell was ghastly. It was everything Shepherd could do to keep his stomach down. It reminded him of the gangrene he had smelled at the mission hospital. He washed the wound and stuffed it with moss.

Quinn spoke first. "That is what I was afraid of…deep infection."

Try as he might, Quinn could not locate the last ball that was mired in Jon's right buttock. He could feel it with his fingers as a lump within the muscle, but he could not find it with the probe. It was too deep. With a sigh of resignation, he cleaned up Jon's back and repacked the wound with the moss. Then he poured some of the pine pitch over each of the bloody wounds.

"We'll have to cauterize the ones that won't stop bleeding," said Quinn, "but I'm afraid to cauterize the one close to his spine. I don't want to take a chance of damaging the nerves there. I might cripple him in some way." He finished wiping down Jon's back before he touched the red-hot knife Shepherd handed him, to several of the wounds, sealing them. He rechecked the dressings then sat down, staring at his patient, going over in his mind what he had done, praying he had not missed anything.

Shepherd threw Jon's ruined shirt into the fire. "No matter how much I'd wash that, it'll never feel clean to me. Quinn, I'm a going to see if I can catch us some trout for supper. I'll be over at the lake."

Quinn put a clean wet cloth over Jon's head and shoulders, hoping to bring down the fever. He couldn't roll him over onto his back because of the dressings and he was afraid the wounds would open. Fortunately, Jon had not awakened during the surgery.

He sat there next to his friend, drinking coffee and fretting about that piece of lead still deep in the flesh of Jon McKinzey's right hip. Mulling over everything he had done, over and over again, trying to remember anything he might have missed. They had packed them with clean moss and pine tar to draw the poison. No, he had done everything he knew to do, except remove that last ball of lead, and he turned that dilemma in his mind again and again. What would he do next?

Jon moaned and moved about, trying to reach the wounds on his back. Quinn had to tie him to keep him from disturbing the dressings.

"Sleep, Jon, sleep. We've done all we can do. You have to do the rest. Let your body heal. Sleep is the best medicine." He changed the cloth, keeping it wet so the coolness would bring down his patient's temperature.

Finally, he simply sat and watched. He had done everything in his power to help. The rest was in the hands of creation.

"How's the patient?" Shepherd came back from fishing with two fat trout, gill-strung from a slender stick. "I'll cook these up in a wink. Do you want biscuits or crackers?"

"Our patient is resting is all I can say. I had to tie his hands, and he's been quiet since then. Help me untie him. I'm worried about the one still in him. If the infection is as deep as the one that ruptured all over us earlier, that infection has to come out. I don't think we can wait. Whatever you want to do for supper is fine with me. I'm not much hungry, but I'll eat something. Make it easy on yourself. The waiting is driving me crazy. Watch Jon, would you? I need to get up and walk around."

Quinn wandered through the meadow to the lake, deep in thought, while Shepherd prepared their meal and kept an eye on Jon. It was a cool evening. They were cocooned in the forest surrounded by old growth spruce and pine. Quinn's face was lost in shadow and doubt as he stretched his arms, trying to refresh his mind and think through what he needed to do next.

Tall cattails and sedges swayed with the evening breezes that came drifting in from the coast, causing ripples across the lake. Sitting on a boulder overlooking the lake, he rolled and smoked a cigarette, watching the ripples lap against the shore, trying to let his mind go blank. He was tired from the mental strain. After scratching his back against an outcropping, he leaned against it for a brief pause and instantly fell asleep.

Something grabbed his toe, and he startled awake, fists balled and ready to fight.

"Supper's ready, pard. Sorry to wake you. What's this a here?" Shepherd picked up a shell bowl filled with pine sap, moss, and charcoal and proffered it to Quinn.

Instantly, Quinn knew what it was and stood to look around. He couldn't have been asleep but a few minutes.

The mysterious shaman had come and gone again, leaving his good medicine next to Shepherd's sleeping body. Nothing moved in the rushes and grasses except the evening breezes brushing them out of her way.

"Hey. Hey out there. Come back. I want to talk to you. Hey!" Turning in all directions, Quinn called and beseeched their benefactor to return.

Silence, then a few birds flew out of the trees off to his right as they had before. Mystery compounding mystery beguiled Quinn as he climbed down from the rock and followed Shepherd back to camp.

"Ain't much. Just some greens and fish. My bannock is a thing of beauty though. Wished I had some honey to drizzle across it. You hungry yet, Quinn?"

"Let me see to our boy here first." In the dimming light, Quinn studied Jon's back. Some of the wounds were scabbing over, and he changed their poultices after adding a bit of the mystery shaman's mixture. Covering the entire back with a washed clean cloth he had soaked, Shepherd noted Jon's hip was red and swollen. With the back of his hand, he could feel the heat deep within the muscle.

"I'm worried, Shepherd. That shot is festering, and I need to get it out. I just don't know if I have the skill to go that deep."

"I seen a doctor in the Army lance a wound to drain it afore he went in to take out a bullet. Used a sewing needle and sinew to sew him up after. Patient was good as new in a few weeks, but they had to keep draining the wound, until he healed up." Shepherd glanced across the camp. "I got a sail needle and sinew in my pack I use to repair everything, from hide to canvas. The sinew should also dissolve in time, won't it? We won't have to go back and remove any stitches, will we?"

"We can only guess. One step at a time." Quinn chewed his lip as his mind churned with questions he couldn't answer.

"Jon still has fever. He's hot, and his skin is clammy. That wound is swelling and getting worse. If we don't do something, he's going to lose that leg or spread infection throughout his entire body. We have to do something, even if it's wrong," Quinn washed the cloth covering Jon's back and replaced it. "Maybe, those sinew stitches would work after all."

"If we start now, we can be done with it by midnight. I'm afraid to wait until morning, like I was wanting to do earlier. The infection is growing. Let's do it now. If this works, it'll be a miracle." Shepherd gestured to Quinn. "Help me tie Jon up so he don't move. If he wakes up while I'm cutting, I might cut him more than I want to, and I don't need that."

They tied Jon in such a way that his knees were drawn up to his chest so he couldn't extend his legs. Quinn no longer could feel the ball under his fingers when he examined him. The pocket of infection was larger. The area was rubrous and swollen.

"Do your best, Quinn. I know you will. That needle and sinew is washed and in the clean bowl."

Quinn nodded. After washing the area, he felt where the prominence of the infection seemed to be. "If I cut straight down here, I should be able to drain everything in one cut."

Perspiration beaded on his brow as he went over his plan in his mind again. "Guide my hand and keep me steady," he prayed. Taking a deep breath, he quieted his mind then made small incisions back and forth with the double-edged blade, digging deeper and deeper.

Jon flinched and tried to pull away, but the ropes constrained him. "Shepherd!" He gasped white-eyed. "What..."

Working deliberately, Quinn cut deeper and was rewarded with a gush of blood and pus that spewed from the incision into the bowl he had placed for that purpose. Using a probe as before, he kept the wound open to let it drain. Jon stiffened and tried to kick back but couldn't, and then he lay still. Quinn cleaned the wound.

"Where's that bottle you offered me earlier?" Quinn sat back and examined his work. Using his fingertips to examine the area where he knew the bullet to be, he pressed to extract more of the infection until the blood oozed clear. "I don't feel anything. There's no lump of a ball where I thought it should be. It must have gone deeper. I hope not. I have to get this out. Here we go."

He kneaded and pressed Jon's back, afraid to go too deep or not deep enough. "Damn, damn, damn."

"Nothing. I can't find it, Shepherd. What'll we do now? For the life of me, I can't feel it with my fingertips." Quinn dropped his tool into the hot water pan. "I don't know what to do. I was so certain this would work."

"Let me clear all of this away." Shepherd picked up the dish, and something rolled around in the bottom. "Wait! Quinn, the ball is in the bowl. Hallelujah!" He got to his feet. "I'm going to dump this and clean up a mite. Wash out the wound as best you can. I'll be right back."

Quinn wiped the area clean. The wound was bleeding free of pus and fluid. He put a pad of moss and pine pitch over it. Jon's backside was proud and bruised from the operation. "Damn, damn, damn. I'm glad that is over. I don't think stitches will hold. The flesh is too bruised. We have to use your knife again."

"You did it, Quinn. You did it."

"Let me get him cleaned up and take off these ropes." The wound looked clean with some mild bleeding. No major vessels had been cut.

Jon jerked, coming to with a wild look on his face as he tried to sit up. "What are you doing to me? Don't do this. Leave me alone." Jon thrashed around, struggling against the ropes, opening up his wounds.

"Jon!" Quinn ordered. "We gots to do this so's you don't bleed to death."

Jon fell back into his blankets, nodding. His eyes told them he knew what they were doing.

"Take a big swalla of this." Quinn offered Jon the bottle and helped him upend it until Jon gasped and sputtered, waving the bottle away.

"Jon. There's one thing more I gots to do. Look up here a minute, will ya?"

Jon raised his head, and Shepherd slugged him point-blank on the jaw, knocking Jon senseless again.

"I had to brand my worst enemy once, and now, I've got to brand my own brother." Shepherd looked to Quinn and back at Jon's bleeding wounds. Knowing he had no choice, he gulped a deep breath, steeled his grip, and touched the red glowing blade to several points on Jon's back. The sound of sizzling flesh chilled him to his marrow. Then it was over, leaving the stench of burned skin and smoke drifting in the air. Shepherd dropped the knife. "I never want to do that ever again." He placed moss and pine tar over the wounds.

"That's all we can do, Shepherd. Now, we wait."

Quinn got to his feet and walked off. He breathed in the cool, crisp breeze in quick, shallow gasps, before vomiting behind a tree. Shaking and so weak, he dropped to his knees, barely managing to support himself to keep from falling into his own sickness.

CHAPTER 16

Sunlight played across the tiny meadow, creeping upon Jon McKinzey's eyelids. He rubbed his eyes, irritated with what had woken him. Where was he? Lying on his stomach hurt his back. Trying to move was worse. Everything hurt. A cloth fell off his back when he rolled over. He couldn't sit, so he tried to stand. There was no strength in his legs. He opted to crawl.

"Whoa, there. You'll start the bleeding. Stop. Stop where you are. Let me help you."

"Shepherd?"

"Yeah. It's me. Lie on your left side. Let me look at you." He knelt to check his wounds. "Damn, boy. It's bleeding. I'll have to repack it. Hold still." When he finished, he sat back on his heels. "Want some coffee?"

Jon nodded. "What are you doing here?"

"Here, drink this. When was the last time you had something to eat or drink?"

Jon shook his head. "I don't remember." He sipped his coffee and looked at Shepherd. "Quinn is with you? This is Quinn's coffee."

"Yes, it is. He's out trying to rustle up a deer or anything he can find. There's biscuits. We ain't got a lot of grub."

"What are you both doing here?" He glanced over to the

camp entrance.

"Where's Derry?"

"He's fine. Horses are loving this meadow grass. There's plenty of water. They're content, right where they are. We haven't even had to hobble them."

"How you feeling? Hurt much?"

"Some. When I move my right leg mostly."

"I'll bet. You were pretty ripped up. We heard about Gold City."

"Who tol' you?"

"Some old Chinese man back at what used to be a town. Someone burned it to the ground. Some down at the stable said they saw what you done and watched you ride out of town. Near burnt up half the town, I hear," Shepherd watched his brother though troubled eyes..

"Accident. The Chinese blocked my way. Their torches set off the fire."

"Well, look who's back among the livin'." Quinn walked out of the woods with a rabbit strapped to a thong around his wrist. He propped up his rifle against a log, hung the doe over a log then squatted to shake Jon's hand. "It's good to see you awake. We've been observing your backsides, mostly. Happy to see your face fer a change."

Quinn poured himself a cup of coffee. He and Shepherd sat gazing at each other. Jon studied them, not making eye contact with him.

The silence grew deafening. Jon could beat it no longer, "What? What do you want?"

"Well...speakin' for myself, an' I suspect Quinn here, I'd be interested to know what the hell you been doin' since I last spoke to you and you left me with the horses."

Jon held their focus for several minutes. "You mean since I last saw you at Trapper's place, and we shot the gang to pieces?"

"Yeah, and there abouts is exactly what I mean." Quinn knelt by Shepherd and both looked Jon in the face.

"Well, Shep. I got chased by some Yoncallas and holed up in a box canyon for four days while they tried to get to me. Broke out by shootin' up their camp, releasing all their horses, and trampling over them as they slept. Rescued a Coos' woman they had captured, but she ran away from me not too far north of here. I found Whitey Nolan, his brothers, Lucky and Steve, in Gold City, hid out for a few days, investigating where they went and what they did. Tracked Lucky and Steve into an opium den, where I hid in wait before murdering them in their beds. I slashed Lucky's throat. Steve, I hung like a Christmas ham. As a remembrance to Pa, I carved MCK on their chests so they would know who done it. I shot Whitey to pieces in the corral and ran all twenty-four horses—some MCK brand, by the way—over him. Got raked by a shotgun at close range. Since then, I killed anything that moved on two legs. The fire in town was caused by a torch one of them Chinese from the laundry dropped, as I pushed him out of my way.

"That's what I've been doing, brother of mine. Landed here three days later, from what you tell me, brought here somehow by Derry. What part of that story would you be interested in?"

"Why, er…" Quinn got up and stretched his back, studying Jon. "Think, I'll go do some more hunting… Did you get it out of your craw, son?"

"'Cept for the dreams at night. I see their faces when I sleep." Jon set down his cup and crawled back into the lean-to with his back to the fire, ignoring them further.

"He's carrying around a lot on his mind, Quinn. Maybe it's best if we just leave him alone for a while." Shepherd collected the cups to wash them.

Quinn looked for young saplings to build a drying rack. After cleaning the doe, he cut strips of meat and salted them before hanging them on the rack to smoke and dry. Neither of the men went far from camp. They always stayed within earshot in case they were needed.

Shepherd checked Jon's wounds without passing a word between them. Jon remained listless and aloof. His back healed in the mountain breezes. Shepherd could see no signs of abscess or inflammation. What was going on in his brother's mind now concerned Shepherd. He did not have the knowledge of how to heal a person's mind.

Stewing venison, cattail roots, and local greens together, Shepherd gave this soup to Jon when he came to the fire that night. No one asked any questions. A heavy silence permeated the camp. The older men did not know what to say, and the younger one remained silent, lost in his own dark thoughts.

Shepherd wanted to wait until Jon was able to ride before breaking the news that they had come to take him back to Oregon City. This business was getting out of hand. He did not want to do this job, but he knew of no other course of action that would not leave Jon a wanted man.

Breakfast was quiet the next day until Jon finally demanded answers. "So, why are you here, Shepherd? I told you this was something I needed to do alone. Quinn, who's taking care of the horses we brought back? You boys didn't just find me in this forest, all shot up. You've been trailing me, I'm sure."

"Horses is fine, Jon. They're back ta home by now."

"They've started work on the mill a few weeks ago, Jon. Thought you'd like to know." Shepherd stood to go.

"So, you came all this way to bring me that piece of news, Shep? The horses are back home; is what you came all this way to tell me, Quinn?"

Shepherd sat down. He held Jon's attention for a few seconds. "We've come to bring you back to Oregon City, Jon. The governor has issued a warrant for your arrest. Lyle Newton deputized me and Quinn to come and bring you back. There's been too many complaints about your shooting up Whitey's gang. The governor is trying to bring law and order to this frontier. Lyle convinced me I was the only one who could bring you in peaceably. That's it. I've got the badge to prove it. We tracked you to this spot, patched you up, and I was waiting for your wounds to heal before I told you."

"Lyle sent you?" Jon scowled.

"The governor did. Lyle's just following orders. He doesn't like it any more than the rest of us. He felt, if you came in, you could clear your name and get this behind you. I wrote a letter to the governor explaining how this all started, but the warrant had already been issued."

Jon rubbed his arms and sat back, glaring at his brother. "When were you going to tell me all this?"

Shep held out both hands in supplication. "Whenever seemed like the appropriate time. This seemed like the appropriate time."

"Who protected my pa? What about John McKinzey?" Jon accused. "Where was the law? Who issued a warrant for Whitey?"

"That's what I explained in my letter. This all started before Oregon was a territory." Shepherd tilted his head, imploring, "Jon, I wanted to go with you to hunt these animals down, remember, brother? I'm only doing this to keep you from being a fugitive and to stop any further killing."

"No promises made? No guarantees? No leniency?" Jon's voice was frosty with derision.

"I'm hoping that there will be an answer when we get back to Salem. I don't like it any more than you. We hope this all gets cleared up. Otherwise, you'll be a wanted man in the territory with a price on your head, and any damn fool with a gun can come looking for you."

"I wasn't thinking of going back." Jon shook his head. "Too many memories."

"Right now, your head is filled with too many memories you're having trouble living with. I hear you at night, fighting them over and over again. Maybe this will help the nightmares end."

"I'll think about it." Jon crawled back into the lean-to, his back to Shepherd and Quinn.

Later that afternoon, Jon crawled out of the shelter, put his hat on, and stood stiffly, looking about. "Shepherd, mind if I borrow your extra shirt and some pants. Mine were all shot up. I feel like going down and checking on Derry. I haven't seen him for a while, and he'll be wondering about me. They're over on the other side of the meadow, aren't they?"

Shepherd nodded. "That's a fine idea, Jon. Careful, you don't open that wound. Derry certainly will like to see you. Can you walk? Should I cut a staff for you?"

"No. I want to do this on my own. Test my balance and such. Feels good to be standing up again. Pretty stiff in my butt. How deep did you have to dig, Quinn?"

"Felt like to China."

Shepherd watched as Jon cautiously limped across the meadow to where the horses stood watching him approach, their tails twitching in the breeze, ears alert, curiosity in their eyes. "That's a good sign. He's up and walking. Seems to be feeling better. Maybe this will turn out pretty good after all."

"Well, I hope so. He's been through a lot. I wouldn't want to go back if'n I was him, but I hope he does. Getting all this behind him is important." Quinn scratched himself under his shirt, squatting on his heels. "I'd like to get settled down for a while myself. Maybe Becky could use a hand at the restaurant, or I could do some scouting for Lyle. I'd take my pay with vittles and pie and a nice bed to sleep in. I haven't seen a bed in months. Forget what anything feels like that's not harder than dirt."

"Yeah, I'd like to get back to a normal routine myself." Quinn pulled down the deer he had shot then sliced the hide away from the body. "Give this badge back to Lyle and tell him to find someone else." When he finished, he flipped his knife into a log then turned to see where Jon had gone.

"Ahem, Shepherd," Quinn interrupted.

"What?"

"My eyesight ain't what it used to be, but would you look over there and tell me if my eyes are playing tricks on me. That shore looks like Jon up on Derry, and he's hightailing it out of here with our horses in tow behind him."

"What?" Shepherd jumped to his feet. "Oh, no. Wait, he's turned around and is coming back."

Jon rode up, trailing the other horses behind him, stopping far enough away that they couldn't rush him. He tipped his hat. "Felt it would be rude to leave and not say goodbye. Appreciate your patching me up. Quinn, I've been thinking over what you told me, and my gut tells me this." Jon held up one finger. "Don't come looking for me. I won't be easy to find." He held up a second finger. "I ain't going back. I don't trust this governor." The third finger joined the others. "I'll live by my own rules. *Adios*." He pulled Derry back around the way they had come, vanishing through the forest, birds flying out of the trees in alarm as they passed.

"By Jehosaphat, I didn't see that a happenin'." Quinn knelt in the dust, pulled a single stalk of grass, and put it in his mouth.

"I didn't, either." Shep blew out a breath. "I'm likin' carrying this badge less and less. At least he left our guns and the camp. He burned down the last place he was in."

"Yes, he shore did at that. I was plumb lookin' forward to that bed and eatin' regular."

Shepherd squatted and brushed his hand over the grass then peered at his fingers. "He's opened his wound. Damn boy. He's bleeding again."

Chapter 17

"So, where is he?" Shepherd stared off into the forest with the Cascade Mountains looming behind. He was puzzled and weary after walking for three days before they found an Indian camp where they could get horses and some provisions. Shepherd had to give up one of his pistols to make the trade.

"I've been chewin' on that question in my mind since we got these horses from that Paiute camp, Shep. He's three days ahead of us, and I can't find no tracks. Where would you go if'n you lost your family?"

"I'm family," Shepherd said.

"No, you're the enemy right now. He's hidin' out and layin' low. Bet he's got a place in mind where he'll be safe and can heal up."

"You're thinking the same thing I am, Quinn. He's headed for Flying Eagle's camp."

"That's just what I was figurin'. The Shoshone are in their own lands. No law there. He can hide out and get hisself right."

"Plus, there's a girl in all of this, as well." Quinn straightened up in the saddle, stretching his back.

"Well, glory be. I ain't heard him talk of no girl."

"I can tell you he has. He's not been around you long

enough. I betcha she's been on his mind. If I was him, that's where I'd be headed. How about you? They should be at their buffalo camp this time of year."

"I think it's the mostest logical place to go look. Now, all we got to do is find them Injuns, in thousands of square miles of mountains and desert. If'n we're lucky, we may cut his trail before then."

"That's what I think, too."

"What say we cut over to the old Oregon trail by following the new Applegate trail that's a goin' south, then cut east until we come to the Snake and head down to Bridger's fort, lookin' for them as we go. Once we're out of the mountains, it's pretty much desert to the Snake. Starvation, no water, and Indians is all we got to worry about."

Shepherd looked puzzled. "Somehow, all that made sense to me. Don't ask me how. You know the way?"

"I jist follow my nose. You follow the rest."

"Yah." Quinn whipped his pony into a long lope.

Shepherd left no doubt of his intentions. Mimicking his guide and friend, he lashed his reins against the back side of his piebald pony and followed what Quinn was leaving behind, space and dust.

Quinn led the way on an old trail the Paiutes pointed out to them that led through the mountains. They moved faster than they could with wagons, traveling northeast toward the Snake and, hopefully, Flying Eagle's camp. As the mountains broke into lower peaks and rounded outcrops, Goose Lake shimmered in the sunlight on their right. Grass was green and lush in these parts with stands of pine bordering fresh clear streams. Lupines and fireweed mixed with goldenrod and blue camas painted the landscape as the mountains became more rolling hills without the craggy snow-covered peaks they had just passed through. It was a beautiful country. Eagles, osprey, hawks, and vultures cruised the sky looking for their dinner either in the water or hiding on the ground. A rich land but ignored as the two men hurried to catch up to the man they hunted. Traveling until the light impeded their progress, they made camp for the night and bedded down next to a small fire built between giant deadfall logs, serving as windbreaks.

Next morning as they broke camp, Quinn told Shepherd over a cup of coffee, "We've got the Cascade Mountains behind us, Shep. Should make better time over these sloppy plains and mountain ridges. At least we got plenty of water."

Shepherd finished his coffee and pulled a piece of jerky warming up over the fire, tossing it back and forth between his hands to cool it before taking a bite. He rolled up his bedroll then tied it to his saddle, mimicking Quinn in doing the same in preparation to leave their camp. "I'm worried, Quinn. We ain't seen any Indians along this entire trail. Are we that lucky?"

"Don't know, Shep. They's been acting up in these parts for a couple for years now, but if it's luck, I'll take it. We're making good time. I reckon Jon to be pretty close. If'n he's losing blood, he should be pretty weak and not fit to ride for long spells. There's been water enough. He would have had to come through these passes. There's no other way 'cept over them."

Shep spat on the ground. "Getting low on tobaccer. Hope we come to some place soon. We're low on everything."

"Plenty of game, hereabouts. I bet we can get a deer or maybe an elk. We've spooked a few already." Quinn set his rifle on the front of his saddle in readiness. "Roasted elk is right up there on my list today. I've had enough jerky and beans on this trip."

◆◦◈◦◆

Green grass and tinkling, flowing brooks and streams

eventually gave way to dryer, browner vegetation and flatter, bleaker landscapes. "We're going into the Oregon desert from here, Shepherd. Not much growing, 'cept sagebrush, rocks, sand, and rattlesnakes. The Hart Mountains, we keep to our left. The Steen Mountains, we'll keep to our right, heading northeast until they open up, and we head farther north looking for hot springs. We'll hole up there for a rest, let the horses graze, and we'll all soak up some of those mineral springs. It'll feel good on my back, that's for sure. Due east of there lies the Snake. Them Shoshones should all be huntin' bufferlo about this time of year. The sooner we get out of this desert, the better I'll like it."

"How far is it?" Shepherd sat his horse eyeing the far horizon without an end in sight, pondering the prospect of the desert crossing.

"Not far. If'n we don't bog down in loose sand pits. Swallow ya up, they will. Waterholes is along the sides of the mountains, if'n there was a good snow. We'll have to look for whatever is green. Four maybe five days, we should be at the hot springs with luck and fast travel. They's antelope, rabbit, and sage grouse out here. Shoot if you see some. Saves time hunting. We'll cook during our noonin'. No campfire at night. Fires can be seen for miles out here."

Sky stretched forever over the Oregon desert. A carpet of sage and twisted branches of salt brush, brave and hardy enough to survive the dry and sun-drenched plain, painted dull grays and greens on a flat palette of sandy brown-and-gold desert, somehow was utterly beautiful. This was broken occasionally by dry lake beds with their white, scaly dried surfaces overlaying soft powdery, long-forgotten lake bottoms. Ancient places, seemingly here since the dawn of time, took them back to before memory was ever thought of.

"Hard to believe, this was all under water long ago."

Shepherd stood in his stirrups to look around, trying to get a vision of what this must have been at some distant time, thousands of years before it all dried up and became this arid. "This is a very, very old place. Now, only antelope and the ghosts of the sacred dead haunt these plains."

Quinn and Shepherd rode quickly, passing the Hart Mountains and heading for the lonesome, vast, protuberances of the Steen Mountains looming on their right. The Steen's were high and mostly flat with fewer, lower peaks. Quinn followed the mountain on the northwest side and kept a sharp lookout for greening willows and cottonwoods, which would indicate a spring or seep.

Two days from the start of their desert trek, they nooned at a spring on the northeast side of the Steen's. A spring pooled at the base of the rock, streaming down a declivity to disappear under another rock, before going underground again. It was hot, and the men took this chance to cool off and let the horses rest, browsing on whatever they could find.

Shepherd had shot a few grouse and a rabbit on the trail. He broiled them over their hot sagebrush fire on a flat rock, adding a little salt and sprinkling some of the prevalent sage that grew everywhere. They had been maintaining a cold camp and a hot meal was welcome. Sharing the grouse with Quinn, he next thoroughly cooked the rabbit. Using a smooth round rock from the stream, he hammered the carcass until it was mashed flat, crushing bones and flesh, salted it, and left it in the sun to dry more over the smoky fire.

"Dried smoked rabbit tonight, Quinn. The sage and salt will make it tasty eating, though a mite crunchy. I'm going over in the shade here and catch a nap. Wake me when you're ready to leave."

"Probably going to catch some shut-eye myself. Hot today. We've made good time. No need to kill the horses.

We'll rest up here until the sun passes overhead and make out for a few hours more riding in the afternoon."

Shepherd made himself comfortable in the small sheltered area out of the sun. He moved a rock to make a place to lie back into when he stopped in amazement.

"Quinn. Come see this here."

"What is it, a snake?" Quinn peered over the side of Shepherd's shoulder so he could see better. "What in the world you got there?"

"Bloody bandages, Quinn. Jon was right here in this spot and changed his dressings and hid them under this rock. Blood is black, so it's been a few days, but we are closer to him than he knows."

"We should be able to pick up his trail from here, if that's the case. Next water is at the hot springs. Good place to hold up and get to feeling better. If I was him, that's where I'd go. Shepherd, if we let the horses rest for a few more hours, we should be able to ride on into the cool of the night and pick up some time on him. Moon is pretty bright. What do ya say? We can camp about midnight and get an early start. Just let the horses go nice and easy. We might surprise him about breakfast or late morning, if I'm readin' this right."

"I think you are, Quinn. Yes. I'm sure of it. These are the last bandages I put on him. See, the poultices have stained the cloth, along with the dried blood. This is Jonny. I know it. He's lost a lot of blood. He won't ride far or fast. I think we can catch up to him."

They waited for the heat of the day to pass before crossing a broad flat panorama of desert, wading through sage and sand. At night, a bright moon cast eerie black-and-silver reflections on the landscape, giving an unworldly,ethereal feel. It took a while for their minds to adjust to the different shadows and hues. Images played tricks on their eyes, and they rode in a state of advanced alertness with their rifles cocked and ready. Exhausted by their long ride and ever-present sense of danger, they decided to stop in the middle of this sea of arid dryness to rest about midnight, giving the horses a much-needed break. Quinn gave each horse some water in his hat and wiped the dust from their noses and nostrils. "They'll be plenty of water tomorrow, boys. This will have to do for now."

There was no place to hide in that vastness, no rocks or trees, only the omnipresent sage, so Quinn showed Shepherd how to pile up sagebrush to make a shelter. "This gives us a place to sleep and be out of sight at the same time. Reminds ya of home, don't it?"

"Right now, bedding down under a wagon seems like luxury to me, but I'll take this over nothing at all." Shepherd smoothed his blankets out and tossed his saddle down for a pillow.

Both were soon asleep under a vast swirling cascade of stars set in the vacuum of an endless universe, accentuated by burning space debris flaming out as shooting stars overhead. Nearby, animals avoided the man smell, leaving the sleepers on an isolated island in the busy skittering highway of nighttime activity. Life and death played out in the age-old way, only by different participants than the daylight shift.

CHAPTER 18

Dawn woke them to a brilliance seeping in through their makeshift shelter. After shaking off their fatigue, they saddled their horses, giving them a precious few cups of water, saving the last drops for themselves. Shepherd handed Quinn several thin strands of smoked rabbit then tore off a piece for himself, like he was biting off a chaw on a long black twist of tarry tobacco.

"That's the last of the food, Quinn, except for a few cups of flour I got left. Canteen's dry, too. How far to these hot springs? We can make a bannock for supper."

"A few hours. At least it is a cooler ride than yesterday. Trouble is, in this desert, he'll see us coming for miles. Unless he's dead or unconscious, we won't sneak up on him. Still want to go on? He ain't a wanting to go back. There may be a fight if I know my man. Whether he takes a shot at us remains to be seen and depends on what his state of mind is."

Shepherd stood up, looking into the desert ahead of them. " Mac always said, 'There are no guarantees,' Quinn. I don't know what Jonny is thinking right now, or even if he can think straight at this point. Either way, I gots to go on. If you don't want to, I understand, but I have to see this thing out."

"He's my friend, too, Shep. I taught him how to live out

in the wilderness, and he's surviving on what I taught him. I ain't givin' up on him or you. Don't know if he's dead or alive, but I'm goin' on. There's too much of a good man left out there to just let him die in this forsaken desert. Hell, this is too much talk. Let's jist go." Quinn spat in the sand and rode on ahead, expecting Shepherd to follow him, as usual.

Silently, the men rode in the coolness of the morning. Their horses nipping at the sage, relishing the few drops of moisture collected on them. In an hour, the moisture was gone, and the heat seeped through the desert in ever-increasing waves of dry heat reflected up off the dust and sand of the dry lakebed. Their hooves raised little plumes of dust with each step, leaving man and beast coated in fine white silica powder. Shepherd rode abreast of Quinn, when a gleaming in the distance caught his eye.

"Crystal Springs is dead ahead of us, Shepherd. We're good targets for anybody with a rifle from any direction out here. Let's jist go slowly, see what happens. His tracks lead straight to the springs. No doubt about it."

Moving slowly, every sense alert, the riders approached, letting the horses find their way through the sagebrush maze. Heat in shimmering waves rose off the distant water like a mirage, backgrounded by hazy blue mountains in the far distance. Vultures rode the heat waves in lazy circles like floating phantoms waiting for death. They were the silent guardians of the desert, filling their niche by keeping it clean.

"I hope those vultures keep to theyselves," Quinn muttered. "I ain't got no use for dying in the desert. Got me some better prospects in mind, but I do feel like a target with a rifle pointing at me. Makes my hair stand up on my back. Never liked that feelin'."

"I don't like it none, neither," Shepherd agreed, standing up in his stirrups looking ahead. "I just hope he realizes it's us, before he goes blasting away. He don't miss very often."

Just as he spoke, a shot shrieked over their heads, startling horse and rider. Both men fought to control their horses. They dismounted, hiding behind their horses, not offering a chance for a target.

"Go away! What are you doing here? I'm not going back. Turn around. I don't want to shoot you," Jon's voice called clearly across the arid landscape. There was no way to tell what direction it came from. Another two shots whistled overhead as a warning.

Remounting, they rode on ahead. Quinn guided his horse with his knees, holding his hands high. Shepherd did the same. Wind gusts picked up from the north, blowing sand and silt in their faces, and they had to shield their faces with their arms and hands.

"I don't want to kill you. Go back home. I...I don't." Jon's voice faded in the distance.

"We don't want to shoot, either, Jon. We're out of water and food. Let us come in, so's we can water the horses and talk," Shepherd yelled over the wind, waving his hands so Jon could see he had no weapon.

There was no reply, except a gust of wind.

Quinn looked at Shepherd. "Let's go around this a ways."

He kept his hands out in front of him with his reins clearly visible. Shepherd did the same. They rode the horses around the dunes until they came to a makeshift camp.

"I tol' you. Go back..." Jon's weak voice struggled to be heard over the blowing wind.

As they neared the camp, no shots were fired. Rounding a short copse of rock bordering the hot water lake, Shepherd found Jon laying on his back against a small declivity in the ridge along the lakebed. His face was white, and his hair was wet. His blood-soaked shirt was matted against his hip. He struggled to sit up, raising his pistol, struggling to pull the trigger.

"I ain't going back, Shepherd." Jon stopped and shook his head. "I... I...can't shoot you." His gun dropped, and his head lulled off to one side. Jon's eyes stared at them in resignation. "Damn it, I can't shoot either of you." His eyes rolled to the back of his head, he collapsed from blood loss and weakness.

Shepherd checked Jon's pulse making sure he was still alive. "Damn fool, brother of mine." He checked Jon's wound and found it was proud and red but not infected. He covered the wound, making Jonny as comfortable as he could. He then straightened up what there was of a camp.

Quinn took the horses to water. Derry greeted them with a nicker. Their horses sniffed at the smell of the water when Quinn tried to get them to drink. Derry drank easily and soon the others followed suit. It was their only choice.

"Water does smell a bit off, but it is water," Quinn told Shepherd. "Glad I don't have any coffee. Wouldn't taste worth a lick anyways." He shook his head at the sorry mess they were in. "I'll get a fire started. How is he?"

Shepherd got to his feet, brushing off his hands. "He's better than he deserves. Lost a lot of blood. He's weak and a bit delirious. He mumbles all the time, like something is going on in his mind, and he's trying to come to terms with it. I've dressed his wounds. Staunched the bleeding again. Looks like the mineral water here has kept it clean. No infection, thank whatever spirits that rule this place. He needs rest, food, and we need to find Flying Eagle's camp."

"Well, let me see if I can lay in a store of meat for ya, and then I'll go find Little Bear and bring some help back here. You get some food into him so's he can take the journey. They's plenty of browse for the horses and of course the water." Quinn blew on the fire until flames danced on the dry branches and twigs. "No water in miles of this place other than this. It just comes out of the ground warm and bubbly like that, stainin' the rocks yella, blue, and green. It's a wonder."

CHAPTER 19

"You really gonna take me back, Shepherd? You'd do that?"

"Don't you see, Jon? You've got to clear your name. You have to go back, or you'll be hunted the rest of your life. Whitey and his gang deserved to die. I wanted to go with you, and I would have been at your side when you did what you did. It didn't work out that way. The times have changed. Laws and attitudes changed. Lyle knew I was the only one to come and try to talk you in, or else some other fella would be lying out there on the desert floor, dying in the heat. You'd have to kill or be killed by whomever they sent. You would have no future. This way, you will have one."

"I will not go to prison. I'll fight my way out if I have to. Better to run and live the life of a wanted man, than to rot in a prison ship or be starved and worked to death in a prison camp. You think of that?"

Shepherd mulled that in his mind for several minutes. "That has been in the forefront of my thoughts from the very beginning. That's what I'm trying to keep you out of."

"I'd rather die. If I am found guilty, I will find some way to escape, even if I have to kill anyone who tries to stop me. A few more on my conscience won't make any difference to me. I saw you in chains. I won't abide it myself."

"I won't see you in chains, either."

"What do you mean?"

"If you are found guilty, and Sam tries to send you to prison, I'll stop him. We brought you in to clear this up, not to have you go to prison. Reason, God willing, will prevail. If you're found guilty, we'll be the McKinzey gang on the run. I won't see you in prison for killing those mongrels. I hope the governor sees it the same way. Here, eat this soup and let's stop fighting between ourselves. I am damn tired of chasing you."

Four days passed before Quinn returned. Little Bear rode with him, alongside five other warriors. Jon was stronger due to the food and what herbs Shepherd could concoct for adding any savor to their meals. He was still sickly from blood loss and experienced terrible nightmares at night. Still so weak he couldn't ride, they put together a travois and hitched it to Derry, who wasn't particularly happy to have this thing tied to him, but when he realized Jon was lying on it, he calmed down and followed Quinn's lead and instruction as they practiced dragging the travois through the brush.

Flying Eagle's camp was off to the northeast. Shepherd tied Jon onto the travois so he wouldn't fall out and gave him a hat so the sun wouldn't burn his face. They rode for four days, following the Owyhee River gorge, during which Jon slept most of the way, disturbed by his dreams and haunted by his devils.

At stops, Shepherd would help Jon off the travois and walk around a little, trying to get his balance back and some strength into his legs. When he put his arm around his shoulders, his patient felt frail, but the color was coming back into his face. Determination and stubbornness kept Jon going.

The Shoshone had come with supplies, blankets, and

coffee. Shoshone hunters kept them supplied with meat, so they ate well. They stopped early in the evenings to rest and water the horses and give Jon a break from the travois.

"Flying Eagle gave me some coffee," said Quinn. "It sure is nice to have some sweet water and a cup of coffee." He had never looked happier.

Jon woke to find Little Bear sitting next to him one morning.

"It is good to see you, my brother. I did not think you could be affected by a white man's bullet. Let's get you up and walk you around. I think we should repeat the blood brother ceremony to increase the strong Shoshone blood in you, and encourage it to flow in your veins and help bring your strength back."

"Sorry to be such a disappointment to you, brother. It is good to look upon your face again. I am not as good as the Shoshone at ducking white men's bullets. I must spend more time with you, so you can teach me how."

Little Bear pulled Jon to his feet and helped him walk a few steps then sat him by the fire, where Shepherd had a bowl of soup waiting.

"Soup again!" Jon groused. "Do we not have any hunters in this party who can bring a joint of meat to this camp?"

"Look who's talking peevish tonight." Quinn cut off a long slice of venison and skewered it on a stick. "Here, boy, cook your own meat. Salts over there. It's time you did something round here besides crawl around on your belly and whine."

Shepherd smiled nodded. Quinn winked at him. This was a good sign.

They entered Flying Eagle's camp at the confluence of the Owyhee and the Snake River. The large camp stretched out along a slough on a broad plain above the river. These vistas and open spaces offered a broad panoramic view, so enemies and buffalo could be seen from miles away. The camp had the river at its back and grasslands to its front. The pony herd grazed downstream of the camp, up on the bluffs, and where they could go down to the river. A good spot.

There was a lodge prepared for the three men, and a few women were assigned to cook and see to the injured Jon McKinzey. Laughing Grass was one of the chosen.

"How ya feelin', boy? That travois shake you up a might?" Quinn tossed his bedroll into the teepee and rolled it out.

Jon was already bedded down, the women bringing him water and bathing his wounds.

"Quinn, I'm feeling weak and sore all over."

"That's good. Show's you're not dead. Dead don't hurt. Looks like they're taking good care of you. I'm going to look around. Shepherd is talking to Flying Eagle, Little Bear, and several of the tribe's elders. They're going to be performing some type of healing ceremony tomorrow night. They're preparing a medicine lodge. You'll be the center of attention here for a while." Quinn chuckled as the women fussed over Jon, and at his dismay as they tried to pull his dirty clothes off him. "They were purty upset you'd been shot."

"Well, tell them to go out, and I'll take these clothes off myself! Hey, don't do that!"

A very persistent older woman successfully pulled Jon's breeches off from his feet and threw them in the fire. Jon scrambled to keep his blankets strategically placed. "Laughing Grass, could you help me? Those were my only pants."

She firmly pushed him back into his robes and began washing his face.

"Seems to me you'll be fine." Quinn stepped out of the tepee, looking for Shepherd. "Good thing he's not feeling hisself. They'd be chasing him buck naked through the camp."

CHAPTER 20

The heat of the setting evening sun faded off Jon's back as Shepherd and Quinn walked with him through the village to the medicine lodge the next evening. He had had his nightmare again last night, so he sat by the fire, not wanting to sleep. Laughing Grass made new buckskins for him. She placed a necklace of turquoise around his neck, telling him it was for protection.

Jon wouldn't let anyone help him walk and insisted on using a stout stick as a cane. He limped with each step but held himself straight, looking ahead. His face was lean and pale, evidence of the physical toll that had emaciated his body. A single leather thong held his long, dark hair tied in place.

Little Bear joined them, wearing a loin cloth and a single eagle feather. He indicated they were to follow him. Women looked up from their tasks and scolded the children who came up to the strangers and touched them with their tiny bows counting coup. Some children made faces but ran away laughing at their own jokes and bravery. Camp dogs eagerly sniffed their legs and had to be kicked away to keep from tripping. Cooking odors changed with each lodge they passed, from roasting meats to the smell of corn charring on wood embers. Men nodded to them in recognition as they passed then joined in behind them. Thus, escorted by the men of the village, the three proceeded to the lodge.

Jon looked behind them as they were about to enter. Twenty to thirty warriors had followed. Their decorum conveyed to the white men that this was considered a solemn event. Everyone stopped when Little Bear stopped. He stood to the side as guardian until everyone gathered at the front of the lodge.

"Shepherd, Quinn, any idea what this is all about?"

"Flying Eagle is going to perform some healing rituals for your benefit tonight."

"But what is he going to do?"

"That we don't know." Quinn hid his voice behind his hand. "When I spoke to him, he was very interested in your dreams and nightmares. Your wounds are healing. He's interested in healing your thoughts, and rejoining the pieces of your spirit together. He says it has been split into many pieces."

"Just trust in Flying Eagle." Shepherd patted his shoulder. "They are doing this for your benefit in their eyes. No harm will come to you." He swallowed and stood tall. "I hope." He gestured to Little Bear that they were ready to enter the grass-walled medicine lodge.

Jon paused by the door flap. "You know what's he's going to do?"

"They call it a peyote ceremony. Some type of spiritual healing ritual, at least that's what Flying Eagle led me to believe when he described the ceremony to me. They use peyote buttons. A kind of cactus for the healing. We all take part. It is eaten, and they make a tea from it. Powerful medicine causes dreams." Shepherd motioned him into the lodge. "Honestly, this is beyond my understanding of healing."

As they entered the lodge, they passed under a huge Bison skull. An older shaman brushed each man with an eagle feather fan from head to toe, banishing any bad spirits that may have entered with them.

Flying Eagle was already seated in his place in the east as head of the ceremony. Jon walked around the fire ring moving to the left, before sitting on the right of the silent Flying Eagle. No one spoke as the rest of the warriors entered and passed around the lodge to the left taking their respective places. There were no women present. Flying Eagle was dressed in white deerskin, beaded with brightly colored designs of birds and flowers. He wore a chest shield make of long hollow bird bones. On his head, he wore a headdress of buffalo horns, holding an eagle feather fan in his right hand and a large gourd rattle in his left, he was the image of a Shoshone Spirit Shaman. His strong face was stoic, calm, filled with humility and a deep peacefulness, evident to everyone.

A single flame burned brightly in the center of the lodge casting flickering shadows across the stern countenances of the seated men. More men moved in carrying drums and rattles, sitting behind the inner circle of men, with their backs against the walls. Bundles of herbs hung from the smoke-stained rafters. Elk skulls, ram skulls, wolf skulls, and other animal skulls adorned the lodge rafters. A raven headdress hung over a bear skull prominently displayed on the west wall. The raven head faced Jon with its body draped over the skull. Painted shields were mounted in the directions of the four winds.

Warm, feral body odors mingled with the smoke and fire from the packed circle of intent men focusing on Flying Eagle as he sat with his eyes closed, his head bowed in prayer. Holding his hands together, palms up, he raised his hands in supplication to the spirits.

A fire tender built up the fire, before placing a large decorated stone bowl filled with water close to the glowing logs. Little Bear passed a pipe wrapped in white wolf fur to Flying Eagle. He gathered a coal and helped Flying Eagle light the pipe.

Flying Eagle gave blessings to the four corners of the earth and offered smoke to the Great Spirit for blessings on this ceremony. Low drumming and rattling accompanied by a shrill vibratory chant echoed from the rings of men. After the pipe was passed around the circle, it was taken away. The fire tender added red cedar logs, strengthening the flames. He sprinkled sage and sweet grass onto the fire, creating a sweet pungent smoke that drifted over the heads of the men before exiting the black smudged smoke hole at the top of the lodge.

Flying Eagle's warm low voice rose above the chanting singing. "He yaa yaa…."

"He is asking for the spirits to heal you. Your spirit has been broken since the death of your father," explained Little Bear as he knelt beside Jon to translate. "He asks the Great Spirit, if it please them, for the spirits to bring healing to you by drawing the broken pieces of your spirit back together so that you may live a fulfilling, meaningful life. Without this healing, he is afraid that your spirit will wander and never find its true path again. He assures the Great Spirit that you have been cleansed before entering this sacred place. You must stand and strip yourself of your clothes and weapons."

Jon sighed in resignation. "What is it with these people and my clothes?" He slowly pulled them off, folding them neatly.

Little Bear firmly pushed him toward Flying Eagle.

Resplendent in his regalia, the Shoshone shaman rose and faced Jon. In English, he spoke, "My son, do you wish this healing to take place?"

The drumming stopped.

"I do, if it is your wish, my father."

"You must be the one who decides this, Jon McKinzey. You must be aware that there are dangers that lurk in the shadows of the spirit world and trust to yourself to make the decisions that will bring the healing power to unite your true spirit."

No one mentioned danger to me!

"What is your desire, my white son?"

"I desire the healing, Flying Eagle. I trust in your guidance."

With both hands, Flying Eagle motioned Little Bear forward. He offered a basket of dried peyote buttons. Flying Eagle indicated Jon should take some. He saw the little amount Jon took and urged him to take more. Flying Eagle indicated he should eat the peyote. Jon took a few more, chewing them slowly to get used to the taste. Little Bear passed the basket around the room, offering each man in turn their part in the ceremony.

Quinn and Shepherd took several as did the other warriors. After offering the basket to everyone, Little Bear poured the rest of the contents into the bowl with the hot water sitting next to the fire, to brew as a tea to be drunk later. The drums and chanting resumed with an urgent intensity missing from the previous session.

Flying Eagle motioned for Jon to sit down. A slow bitterness crept into Jon's mouth, causing him to salivate. He started to spit it out, but Little Bear looked him in the eyes and slowly shook his head. Jon sat and swallowed, trying to ignore the taste in his mouth. He did not want to embarrass Flying Eagle or any of his adopted tribe. Cedar and sage smoke mingled with sweaty man smell, creating a heady aroma all to itself. Moving the coals in the fire around with a stout stick, the fire tender formed the coals into a glowing raven pulsating with heat like an illuminated spirit creature.

It was close in the room. Jon felt a flushing, like a fever wash up his body. Sweat dripped off his nose to the ground. Everyone was watching him, he felt. He wiped his forehead then smiled in reassurance and remained still. His mouth tingled. The taste wasn't so bad. He felt nothing except the heat and smelled the gamey atmosphere of men sitting too close together to be comfortable. It was almost too much, and his stomach threatened to revolt. Then it didn't. Little Bear gave him some water laced with honey and pine needles. That was better. He swayed a little to the drums, wondering if anything was going to happen. The drumbeat was soothing. Chants receded into a dull background noise, rising and falling with each breath he took. Cedar and sage wafted overhead, lulling his mind. His mind drifted.

Jon snapped back to attention. *How long have we sat here?* He felt he was in a sort of trance, lost in the drumming and chanting.

Some of the men began yipping. First one then another. Some sat with tears running down their faces. Flying Eagle sat with his eyes closed. Firelight illuminated his face, smooth and flawless as carved ivory. One man got up and danced in place a few minutes before turning and dancing around the circle. A few more joined him. Jon swayed to the rhythm of the beating drums, watching the dancing, singing men circle the room, their movements creating strange forms cast by the firelight onto the walls. Shadows and light falling across the shields on the wall reminded Jon of a pulsing lightning storm flashing on and off, causing him to blink in time to the dancing light. Little Bear sat back in the shadows, observing Jon and his companions.

The black-eyed raven perched on the bear skull on the west side of the lodge caught Jon's attention. This raven stared at Jon for the longest time, never turning its gaze. Jon could not take his eyes off the shiny eyes and visage of the bird's face. The bird twisted to groom itself. Running one feather at a time between the jaws of his beak, it preened its flight feathers before fluffing and shaking all the feathers into place. It turned its head 360 degrees, then its eyes rolled back into its head. When they rolled forward, they were blue as turquoise, looking at Jon with laughter in them.

"Ready, Jon," the raven said distinctly. That turquoise hew glowed all about its body and neck, haloing his head.

The bird fixed its steely eyes on Jon, and all the rhythms, shadows, and vibrations in the room stopped. Everything in the room expanded, then, in a blink, it condensed, jolting into Jon's psyche, punching him in the chest like a fist.

Jon jumped. "What!"

He looked around the room. No one paid him any attention. Shepherd and Quinn had leaned against one of the lodge poles and were fast asleep.

Little Bear handed him a cup of tea from the fire. "Drink this quickly."

Jon thanked him and drank from the cup, still bewildered by what he thought he had seen. The brew was bitter, but Jon gulped it down, all the while transfixed by the preening raven perched above him at the far end of the lodge. Fascinated, Jon dropped the cup and crawled on his hands and knees toward it.

Raising its left claw, the raven scratched up under its chin. It shook its neck to smooth the disturbed feathers then blinked. "I asked you if you were ready."

"Who me?" Jon looked around. He did not see any other person in the lodge.

Raven ignored him. Turning around on its perch, it stretched and flexed its wings and flapped them a few times then peered down at Jon, waiting for his answer.

"Yes. I'm ready."

"Then let's go!" Raven flew off its perch, under the buffalo skull adorning the door, and out the lodge flap into the unknown.

"I'm coming!" Jon chased the bird out of the lodge and into the blackness. The night sky was a three-dimensional hologram of depth and color. All the power of the universe radiated from the stars. The moon radiated a shaft of silver-blue luster, illuminating the earth in a spiritual glow indescribable to Jon's mind. Everything was so clear. He stood on a grassy plain as soft as doeskin. Never had he felt such elation. Blood raced through his veins, and he could see it flowing beneath his skin, running through the veins and arteries. Pulsing life reverberated through him.

Spirit Raven sat on a thick branch of a silver maple tree, continuing its grooming.

"Hello, I'm here." Jon looked up ataven. He couldn't take his eyes off it.

"Let's begin."

Spirit Raven stretched its wings, and the sky turned black, frosted with an eerie orange light that emitted enough of a low glow that he could barely see. From the far horizons, silhouettes of the mountains loomed, outlined in glowing orange. A force gathered, rolling toward Jon with the strength of an exploding volcano, blasting down the mountain, seeking him out.

Jon sensed this force had a purpose...to catch and destroy him!

There was no place to hide. He panicked and ran for his life. Howls of the dead within the rolling force shrieked for his blood. A large shape formed at the front of the maelstrom. Jon's nightmares had become real. Whitey was alive! All the men he had killed in his life were gathered in that storm, bearing down on him helpless and alone.

A wolf spirit joined him, running alongside.

"Can you help me, Spirit Wolf? They are coming for me and mean to destroy me."

"I can only run by your side. I cannot help you alone." The two ran on.

A snake spirit joined them, running alongside.

"Would you help me, Spirit Snake? They are coming for me and mean to destroy me."

"I can only run by your side. I cannot help you alone," hissed the snake. The three ran on.

An elk spirit joined them, running alongside.

"Would you help me, Spirit Elk? They are coming for me and mean to destroy me," panted Jon Rio.

"I can only run by your side. I cannot help you alone." The four ran for their lives, away from the cloud of certain doom rolling down on them.

On the horizon, a bedazzling light shown, growing closer and brighter. Their fears lessened the nearer they got to the light. It seemed they ran for a long time to reach the light. Running was difficult, like churning through soft ankle-deep mud. It took great determined effort to move forward. Finally, Jon spotted a woman and a man in the light radiating a rainbow of colors creating the white glow and melting the darkness around them as they strode forward. They felt familiar. He ran toward them, their warmth of undying love drawing him forward and encompassing him with strength.

"Can you help me, my parents?" Jon cried.

"Run into our arms, full of love and forgiveness. Together, we can do all things. Heal all wounds." The pair opened their arms, and the light expanded and grew brighter.

First went the wolf leaping into the light, followed by the snake and the elk spirit, and finally Jon plunged ahead. All fell into the loving parental embrace of his parents, who covered them in their pulsating white light, wrapping them in celestial beauty and profound love.

Jon awoke alone but discovered strength radiated throughout his mind and body.

Raven alighted on a nearby tree. "We are not done with you yet. Even though the pieces of your spirit have been brought back together by unbounded love, the bonds are not secure. You have to choose to return to life, or you may choose to continue here." Raven flew to him and beat him with its wings, clawing at his face with its talons.

Jon fought him off, grabbing at the feet as they scratched his face. One of the talons pulled off, and the bird flew away.

"Remember me," Raven called over his shoulder, soon becoming a black dot against the sky, until there was a flash of turquoise, and it vanished.

"What did he mean by that?"

Sensing a malevolent presence behind him, Jon turned. Whitey's face loomed over him in the storm cloud of lightning and tornadic winds, threatening to suck him in.

Panic struck Jon, and he fled. As he ran, he passed a deep cleft in the rocks, emitting a warm-blue light beckoning him in. "I would be warm there. I would be safe." Yet, he hesitated.

Out of nowhere, Flying Eagle appeared, pushing him away, toward the apparition of Whitey and the tempest. Wind whipped Jon's hair as the storm blew stronger. Jon turned to flee into the cave, but Flying Eagle blocked the way screaming soundless words. Pushing and pointing toward the tempest.

"I cannot do this alone," he shouted to Flying Eagle.

"I can help," said the spirit of the wolf from inside of him. "I am cunning and fearless."

"I can help," said the spirit of the snake. "I am wise and patient."

"I can help," said the spirit of the elk. "I am strong and can run forever."

"We are together at last and nothing can defeat us when we act together, bonded by selfless love." All thoughts came to Jon at once. Their hearts beat as one in rhythm and strength.

"You cannot challenge me," said the Whitey spirit. "I will have you now!" The tempest struck in full force, but Jon stood, rooted to the ground like a rock, unyielding to his trepidation.

"I am not afraid any longer. I have the strength of the elk, the cunning of the wolf, the wisdom of the snake, and the power of eternal love. You have no power over me or mine. Do your worst. I defy you!"

"Fear me! I have you." The tempest roared, crashing against Jon, but he would not be moved. It became easier and easier for him to resist the swirling winds and rain. After a time, he laid down upon the soft grass and went to sleep, oblivious of the wrath of Whitey and his ilk.

Slowly, he sank into the ground. He felt everything below the surface of grasses and rocks. He instinctively knew the way the world had formed from a single thought. He understood the pattern of Mother Earth. He could see between the grains of sand and watch the tiniest creatures that lived in the very earth, dependent on the nourishment she provided. These lessons played through his mind, and he knew, without question, that all life was dependent on a pulsing vibrational heartbeat creating all things coming from the center of the universe. Peace permeated his being. All questions were answered.

He bounced back into his body stretched out on the floor of the medicine lodge. A woven robe covered him.

Dazed, unsure of what had happened, he sat up. Flying Eagle's eyes bore into his.

"You have returned, my son?"

Jon crawled around the lodge, getting his bearings. The still form of the raven headdress on the bear skull, sightlessly stared back, head cocked to one side. He didn't remember the head tilt. Confused, he rubbed his eyes. Something in his hand scratched his face, and Jon choked back his astonishment at the fresh raven's claw he held. He turned to Flying Eagle.

"It is the gift he gave to you. He chose you. Raven spirit is strong."

"How do you…"

"Come. The rest are feasting in celebration of your healing. The women have prepared a meal. You slept into the morning. You must be hungry from your journey." Flying Eagle rose, holding the leather flap open, letting in bright sunshine, and gestured for Jon to leave before him.

Laughing Grass greeted him when he stepped out of the lodge. All night, she had kept her vigil.

"Good morning, Jon. You look puzzled about something. Are you happy to see me? Come eat with us." She frowned. "Oh, your face! I'll clean it for you."

"What are you talking about, Laughing Grass? What's wrong with my face?" He raised his hand to feel his skin.

"No. Stop. You'll bleed."

"Bleeding? What do you mean?"

"Jon, you have talon scratches on your face."

CHAPTER 21

Laughing Grass seldom left Jon's side, except when they went to their individual lodges at night. They walked along the river, talking in broken Shoshone and fragmented English. Laughter was their universal language, and they spoke it well. In the quiet pools, they swam naked and exposed to the open sky, relishing each other's nearness. Their lovemaking seemed natural, unrestrained, explosive, and then they held each other entwined, at peace, cradled on some beach or grassy bank, until it was time to return to the camp.

She dabbed ointment on his face to heal the scratch marks that left thin, almost-indiscernible scars. She fueled the energy of his healing of body, soul, and mind, replacing the dark memories with love and a hunger for a bright future.

One day, they sat alone while she weaved a basket. Smiling, like she hid a great secret, she placed a smaller, beautifully decorated, sweetgrass basket in front of him. A raven's image had been woven onto the top cover.

"What is it?" He opened the basket to find a yellow, softly tanned leather bag, laced with a red corded leather tie.

She picked up the soft leather bag and pulled it open. "It

is a medicine bag. You must keep it with you always. You put your talisman in it, to keep it close to your heart. You must have it at the time of your death, so you will not be lost. Indian children keep their umbilical cord with the other spirit totems they receive over their lifetime. Put what you received during your journey in the bag. I will turn so I don't see."

"Laughing Grass, you know it is a raven's claw." He held her hand. "I showed it to everyone." He pulled the talon from a pouch on his belt. "I still don't understand how I had it in my hand. I never left the lodge, I don't think." He placed it within her palm and closed her fingers around it.

"Only you should know what your animal spirit token is." She placed it back into his hand. "We'll pretend no one knows. Put it in your bag and anything else you may receive that brings magic to you."

"All right, if you say so." He smiled, amazed this wonderful woman cared so much for him. With great care, he dropped the talon inside the token bag.

"Flying Eagle says so. Little Bear says so. The tribe says so. It is our way. You are one with us. I will teach you. Understand?"

"What do I do with it?" He tossed it in his hand like a small ball, catching it adroitly.

She caught it on the next toss and put it back in his hand, closing his fingers around it. "When you are in need. You call upon your animal spirit to help you or to guide you out of trouble. Hold it in your hand and sing to it. At the time of your death, you will sing your death song while holding it close to your heart."

"I don't know a death song." He slid over to her, enjoying the nearness of her body. He couldn't help but be aware of her hair, her smile, the way she smelled of smoke, of the mountains, of life itself.

"I will teach you mine," she whispered. "Perhaps we can

talk some of the elders into singing their song and you can make up a song that suits you. Maybe Little Bear will sing you his. It is a very serious and private ritual. Do not be offended if they refuse. I brought a leather thong so you can wear your medicine bag like the other warriors. Here, give it to me so I can tie it around your neck." After receiving the bag, she turned her back to him and reached into her bodice, retrieving a braided locket of her hair which she placed within the medicine bag. She then laced the thong through it.

"Okay, I'm ready. Go ahead." He turned his back to her and lifted his hair out of her way so she could tie the medicine bag around his neck.

"Don't be impatient, Jon. I want this to fit correctly." She swung the loop over his neck and fastened it with a firm knot. "There. Now you will have protection." She beamed with warmth and gave him a hug.

A lone rider galloped into camp, scattering the camp dogs, raising a cacophony of barks and growls, alerting the entire camp, causing everyone to come spilling out of their lodges to hear his news. Jon and Laughing Grass ran with the rest, feeling it must be important.

"Bozheena!" Pointing his bow to the northeast, the warrior stood up on his pony so everyone could see.

"What's he saying, Laughing Grass?"

"He is saying the buffalo have come."

The camp moved en masse with one mind. After grabbing bows, arrows, and knives, the men rushed to the pony herds. They quickly daubed their faces with paint. Every design meant something to the individual warrior. The women changed into work clothes and brought out knives and parfleches to carve and gather the meat. Butchering was a bloody business.

Laughing Grass left Jon, in search of Quiet Woman.

Little Bear came up to him. "Can you ride, my brother?"

"I can. What do you want me to do?"

"Watch how a warrior gets meat for his camp then do the same. Shoot the *bozheena* behind the shoulder if you can. A quick death wastes less meat. The women will do the rest. Come. Flying Eagle is leading the people to the herd. Get your horse."

Jon joined Quinn and Shepherd in saddling their horses.

"I've heard about this, Jon. Never thought I'd get to participate." Shepherd was caught up in the fever of the hunt. He pulled his rifle from the scabbard and checked it. He then removed his shirt and tossed it over in front of their lodge. Other warriors were naked above their waists as well.

Little Bear motioned them over. He had several pots of paint—white, black, red, and yellow. "Paint your faces so the buffalo will not know you." The white men moved over to him with questioning looks.

"I'll do it for you. We do not have much time."

Demonstrating, Little Bear applied black paint to his hands and, using his fingers, pulled down the length of his face, leaving black stripes to his chin. He dabbed his eyelids with red paint and covered his chin in white. He rubbed his hands together, mixing the paint he had, then added red and applied it to Jon's face, then Quinn's. Rubbing his hands together, mixing the paint, left a black hue. He motioned to Shepherd.

Shepherd shook his head. "I'll do mine." He dipped his fingers in the white paint and stroked his face with his fingers, then the red, then the yellow, leaving his face brilliantly striped.

"It is good." Little Bear leaped upon his pony's back, yelling a shrill cry. "All who hunt *bozheena*, ride with me." He rode off, leading a trailing band of excited, animated warriors up the hill to where Flying Eagle waited with his gathering tribe.

Flying Eagle shook his lance in the air and pointed to the northeast. *"Bozheena. Bozheena!"*

Echoing calls came back from the clan that had gathered. *"Bozheena! Bozheena! Bozheena!"*

Turning to the northeast, Flying Eagle led his warriors off at a gallop, leaving the women and children to drag travois full of what they would need for the huge job ahead.

Jon rode up next to Little Bear and Flying Eagle, looking over a vast herd of shifting black forms moving as a flock of birds would. One side flowed one way, merging into another flow, as the herd ate its way across the nurturing native grasses. It was a mesmerizing sight, to behold such a mass of moving bodies.

"Pick an animal, Jon. Try to separate him from the herd and shoot close behind his shoulder. Pull away after your shot so you do not get tangled in his feet and go down."

"What next?" Jon stood in his stirrups, watching the herd.

"Go find another! *Ya heee!*" Little Bear was off like a shot, running down a nearby cow. He guided his pony with his knees, riding low over his mount, holding his bow and arrows in his hands. He held three extra arrows in his bow hand so he could quickly retrieve one and fire again. The cow disappeared under the rolling clouds of dust and dung.

Jon whistled to Derry and bolted after his friend. He held his rifle across his knees. Derry flew like a spirit from hell, joyful at running free. His mane whipped back in Jon's face, and the two of them ran alongside the herd. His first shot missed due to Derry stepping onto a slight rise, shortening his stride, and throwing Jon off-balance. Instinctively, he tightened the grip of his thighs and righted himself. He quickly pushed the rifle into its scabbard and pulled one of the Colts, something he had practiced doing on horseback many times. Nearby, a young bull cast his eye up at the strange apparition running at his side.

Jon leaned over, aimed his shot behind the beast's shoulder, and fired. Derry swerved to the left, away from the herd, giving Jon a chance to find another. When he was ready, he turned Derry toward the herd, bringing him close to a large cow, bawling and grunting as she ran. He fired his first shot, and she staggered but kept running. Jon put another shot into her. She fell in a cloud of dust. Legs and hooves flailed about for a few seconds, stiffened, and lay still. Jon missed his next two shots as a result of being bumped. He swerved several times to keep from being trampled by the maddened herd trying to run from the devils chasing them.

He was able to bring down another bull before running out of bullets. He edged Derry off to the side of the flowing animals, grabbing for his other rifle. The herd thundered on, leaving their bloodied dead in the wake of trampled grass and churned earth. A strange quiet settled in their wake, as deafening as the pounding bawling herd. Jon shook his head to clear his ears.

Now, it was the women's turn. From the perimeter of the killing field, a gleeful ululating cry emitted from the throats of the tribal women as they descended onto the scene, armed with knives, escorted by the children dragging travois loaded with skin bags, jugs of water, and woven baskets to collect the meat and select pieces.

Shepherd rode up. "That was the most exhilarating, frightening thing I've ever done. I can't wait to do it again. I got two."

Quinn waved from the other side of the valley, letting them know he was alright. He turned his horse and headed for them.

"How many do you think we killed?" Shepherd turned in his saddle, surveying the scene. "Looks like every buck got at least one. I got two. You say you got three. There may be forty, fifty kills, it looks like to me."

Little Bear skidded to stop in front of the men. "Well done. Come with me. We must celebrate your first kill as a member of the tribe of Shoshone." He led the way to where Quiet Woman and Laughing Grass butchered Jon's first kill. The women were smeared in blood as they hacked at the skinned-out carcass of the bull lying on its own hide. Little Bear leaped off his pony, gesturing for the two to follow. Quinn pulled up, dismounted in one leap, and joined them.

Laughing Grass watched him as he approached. Joy and pride shown in her face as her hunter returned to his kill. With a cry of victory, she cut open the abdominal cavity, expertly cutting out a hunk of the bloody liver. She sliced off a piece and handed it to him, before cutting off pieces and handing them to the warriors of her family, first Little Bear, next Shepherd, Quinn, and then for herself and Blue Moon.

Little Bear bit and tore off a chunk of his warm, pulsing treat. Then indicated that they do the same.

"It's still hot to the touch, Jon," Shepherd murmured.

The meat in Little Bear's hand steamed in the crisp morning air.

"So's mine. Look like you love it. We don't want to insult anyone." Jon smiled and held his piece up for Little Bear to see. Facing Laughing Grass, he tore off a big bite, chewed it up a few times, and swallowed. "Just like oysters, back home in Indiana, Shepherd. Remember? Pa used to bring them to us when a fresh shipment came into town. Slurp it down. Gotta be good for you."

Beaming, Laughing Grass also tore into her portion with a blood-stained smile as they shared this ancient rite practiced by the tribe, since time immemorial. She wiped her hands on her thighs and motioned him to back away. It was time to go to work.

The men returned to camp and cleaned up, bathing in the river. They would spend the next few days recounting their bravery and how treacherous the *bozheena* were and difficult to bring down. Jon's shooting was praised. Not every man could bring down three *bozheena*. His Colts were envied.

Women and children were left to butcher the meat, build the drying racks, scrape the hides, and make jerky and pemmican for the long cold winter looming ahead. It was a bounteous hunt and would feed the camp well into the winter.

Later, Shepherd and Quinn found Jon coming out of Flying Eagle's lodge.

"Er…" Shepherd grimaced. "Jon, we need to talk to you."

Jon's elation vanished as he read their faces. "It's time to go?"

"It's time to go." He nodded. "I hate to leave this as much as you, but it still remains to be done. Let's put it behind us and come back here one of these days. I haven't felt this freedom since I was back in Indiana living with Pa. We have meat. With extra ponies, we can make double time getting back to Salem and be done with it. Hell, they may have forgotten about you by now."

Jon cocked his head. "You think they may have forgotten?"

"No. No, I don't. I wish it were true, but we have to go and find out. Now is the time to start. It will be changing seasons soon, and I don't want to be out in the winter cold."

"It's the best thing to do. I'm afeared if we don't get back there, they'll send t'others to do it." Quinn squinted at Jon. "I knowed you got something here that makes you want to stay. That's why we need to go. If you stay much longer, you won't go. I understand that."

Reluctantly, Jon acquiesced. He was healthy, in heart and mind as well. His body was strong again. He vowed to himself, if he lived, he would return, or die trying. They said their goodbyes that evening to Little Bear's family, explaining what they must do to finish Jon Rio's full return to men and the society they had left.

Laughing Grass said her goodbyes privately, no tears, but the spirit of the young woman dulled that evening. She had seen white men come into camp, take women for their wives, and never return. It was the way of men. It was the way of whatever ruled the behavior of all things. She left the lodge after the goodbyes and didn't come back. Quiet Woman went to her.

Flying Eagle sat at the fire, expressionless. After his daughter and wife had left, he passed the pipe around the circle as a final gesture.

"I believe you will return to us as soon as you are able, my son. I see it in your heart. A woman's feelings rule her heart. She will understand, with time, why you must do this journey to free yourself from the white man's law. She misses you all ready. Shoshone law would reward you for striking the killers who murdered your father. We will celebrate your return to us. Do what you must."

Early morning found the three men on the trail again, leading several horses and pack ponies. Jon rode Derry. Shepherd rode to his right and Quinn to his left. They traveled light and fast.

A black dot flew in the sky, preceding them, leading the way.

"Is it me, or are your Colts missing, Jon? I see your holsters are clear. You got them in your bedroll?"

"No, you're seeing clearly. Presented them to Flying Eagle as bride price for Laughing Grass. I have a future there. I will come back."

CHAPTER 22

They crossed the great Oregon desert unmolested, arising before dawn and riding until dusk. Trails began to emerge as they neared the mountains. Wagon tracks wound their way to the Willamette Valley before joining the Applegate trail in the Rogue Valley. They saw no one. The routine of the trail coalesced them into a unit of one mind, one body. They were accustomed to each other by now, and each knew what the other would do in any given situation.

Jon still carried his rifle across his saddle. Quinn and Shepherd had their sidearms and knives as well. Quinn scouted most of the time, as he was more familiar with the country. Shepherd followed, and Jon brought up the rear. This formation rotated occasionally, allowing for Shepherd and Jon to learn and gain experience from the territory. Jon remembered very little of it from the time he had passed this way before.

They were near to the southern part of the Applegate trail when Shepherd came riding hard and fast to Quinn and Jon.

"Whole lotta trouble up ahead. Group of wagons being attacked by Indians. Appears like they got bushwhacked. They aren't circled up, but then again, not much room to circle on these narrow trails and forest. Indians are in the trees and hard to see. Looks like they've been pinned down two, maybe three days."

"Let's go survey the situation. I don't want to go bustin' in until we see where everybody in this fight is and isn't." Quinn led the way, cautious of what lay before them.

Gun blasts echoed through the forest as they neared the fight.

"Shotgun," said Quinn." Let's pull off over ta' here and see what goes on."

Breaking off the trail, Shepherd rode between trees and thick brush until he could get a clear picture of the scene before them.

"Just like I left 'em. Six wagons pulled up parallel to each other, giving some protection from the attackers in the forest." Shepherd's horse blew through his nose, nervously shuffling his feet and moving about. Pulling on his reins, he jerked his horse's head back. "Whoa, whoa. What's wrong with you?"

Two brown bodies dropped from the branched canopy above them. Others leapt from the underlying thick cover armed with spears and war clubs, ululating their war cries.

Derry kicked a brown body as soon as it stood up, sending him rolling down the hill, landing in the cold clear freshet at the bottom. The cold water did nothing for the brave's recovery.

"Yoncallas!" Jon swung his rifle butt at the nearest head.

The warrior ducked in time and came up over on the other side of Derry. Shepherd cracked that warrior over the head with the barrel of his rifle before firing at one trying to wrestle Quinn's rifle away from him. He missed.

Quinn pulled his gun away from the young warrior and fired point-blank into his chest, causing him to scream and fall, clutching his life's blood as it pulsed out of his chest. He faded under the greenery to die, thrashing his legs in the brush.

A spear missed Shepherd's head, sticking into a spruce tree, quivering. He threw his rifle at the assailant. Drawing his pistol, he shot the warrior in the arm, missing his mark due to the skittish horse jumping about, fouling his aim.

The last Yoncalla ducked behind a tree when Jon fired his gun at him, nicking the tree near where his head had last been.

"Time to go!" Quinn shouted, waving them toward the wagons.

"Wait. Cover me. I need my rifle." Shepherd jumped off Rocky and retrieved his gun. "Whoa, boy. Now, I see why you were so nervous." Scrambling onto his horse, he waved his rifle toward the wagons. "Go. Go!"

Storming down the hill, Quinn, Shepherd, and Jon burst through the forest to the bottom of the hill at the same time, making for the protection of the wagons.

"Don't shoot. Don't shoot. We're friendly!" They rode between the wagons, stopping in the middle, arms held high so the pilgrims could see they were not Indians.

All three ducked for cover and began reloading their weapons.

"Who's in charge here?" Quinn snapped at the closest man to him.

"Reverend Hopkins." The man gestured. "Over there under that wagon. He's been shot. His wife, Doris, is a-doctorin' him now."

"Who are you?"

"Brother Richard Morse. Where'd you come from?"

Both men ducked as a shot splintered the side of a wagon a few feet away. A shotgun blast returned the call, shattering leaves and branches from where the smoke from the shot still hung in the air.

"If Hopkins is wounded, who's calling the shots around here? You're sure in a pickle." Quinn spit under the wagon as he surveyed the plight they were in. There didn't seem many bright spots to him.

"We've been pinned down for two days. Two killed, two wounded, and one woman stolen away. Haven't had no fire and only raw bacon and flour to eat." Morse fired his rifle into the forest.

"Jon! Shepherd! They got bacon," Quinn called out to his friends, who turned to look at his position.

"Ya don't say." Jon smiled then fired at a feathered head crawling from a bush to a tree. "Got him."

"And flour, Shep. They got flour."

"Ask these nice folks if they don't mind sharin' with the likes of us if we get 'em out of this mess."

"We'd be right thankful to you for runnin' these Injuns off. What ya' plannin' to do?" Brother Morse held the hope Quinn would lead them out of this trouble they were in.

"Any cattle left?"

"We got a milk cow and a one-year-old heifer."

"They yours?"

Shots rang out, hitting a wash tub on the side of a wagon. Mrs. Hopkins threw her body over her husband to shield him as bullets dusted the earth near him, throwing dirt in his face.

"Well, yes, they are. They're yours if it will get us out of this predicament. What ya thinkin' on doin'?"

"We're going to surrender, Mr. Morse." Quinn grinned. "I don't suppose any of the brothers has a bite of t'bacca? I ain't had any chew in a while. Ran out of Indian tobacco a few days ago. Fightin' Indians makes me want a chaw real bad. Got anything white? Indians honor a white flag."

"Nadine! Toss me a piece of your petticoat if you could, please. A big piece."

"What do you want my petticoat for, Brother Morse?" She frowned. "It's the only one I have left. I don't want to be showin' my petticoats to strangers in our midst."

"Just tear off some from the bottom. If not, the Injuns will get it anyways, sooner or later." Quinn covered his eyes with one hand then held out the other. When nothing

151

happened, he peeked between his fingers.

Nadine stared at Quinn, not sure what she should do.

Quinn dropped his hands to his sides. "Lady, I can stop all this, but I need a piece of your petticoat to do it."

Nadine's cheeks pinkened. She flapped her hand at him. "Well, turn your face."

Quinn turned away and was rewarded with the sound of tearing of cloth. Then a wad of white petticoat fell across his hat. "Thank you, ma'am."

Quinn tied the cloth around the tip of his rifle and waved it in the air. "Remind me, Brother Morse, before I go palaver with the Yoncalla, how this all started?"

"We killed a young brave by mistake. Reverend Hopkins took him for a deer in the forest."

It grew quiet. A white flag waved down the trail. Several Indians crept out of the woods, looking toward Quinn.

"Oh, Lordy. Now, what do I do." Quinn stood up and stretched his back, waving his flag at the waiting group of Indians. "I hope he t'weren't a chief's son he shot."

Sobs came across from where Mrs. Hopkins was tending to her husband. "He's dead!" she wailed. "Those murderin' devils killed my husband." She collapsed, crying over the top of Reverend Hopkins.

Nadine crouched low and ran over to the distraught woman's side to comfort her.

"Shepherd, you come with me. Jon, stay here and take care of these folks. I'll go see what can be done to appease the Yoncalla." Holding the flag over his head, Quinn approached the group of Indians. He approached with caution, watching both sides of the forest wall. After all, one of their young had been killed. It didn't pay to believe you knew what Indians would do. They didn't think like white folks.

"Shepherd, watch these boys," Quinn said under his breath. "There's been a lot of trouble here recently, due to the white folks being ugly with the locals. These Yoncallas resent the intrusion, but the pilgrims feel they can do just as they did back home. It's cost lives on both sides."

Jon reloaded his guns while keeping an eye on the men talking down the trail. The folks on the train gathered around their fallen leader and did their best to comfort the new widow. Doris Hopkins was beside herself with grief.

After coming all this way, watching her husband die in her arms, leaving her virtually alone in the wilderness. That realization was awakening deep fears she had kept bound up within her. Those civilized restraints fell apart, and there was nothing she could do to control the horrible actuality of her still-warm dead husband lying in front of her. Feeling helpless, alone for the very first time in her life, a fearsome specter never imagined until now, welled up inside of her, filled her with uncontrolled anger, confusion, and a deep sense of betrayal. Several women tried to console her, but she wouldn't have it.

"It's easy for you to say, 'It'll be all right, Doris Hopkins.' You've all still got your men! God will find a way," she snapped at the women. She pushed them away then turned, facing the throng of men trying to negotiate peace.

"Blood-thirsty savage beasts! I hate you." She stood, fists clenched, screaming louder and louder. "God hates you. I ask him to bring his vengeance down on your heads and destroy all of you blaspheming animals!"

Doris Hopkins lost her sanity in that moment. Grabbing the first thing she could lay her hands on, a broom poking out of the front of a wagon, she charged the group of astonished Indians. Screaming like a banshee out of an old faery tale, she swung the broom at their heads, forcing them to duck and run behind trees, rocks, anything they could find to protect themselves. Relentlessly, mercilessly, she hit them and beat them with her broom, berating them in old biblical damnations, scattering them in all directions.

Finally, Quinn was able to grab her from behind and

hold her still. She collapsed in a fit of laughter and uncontrollable weeping. Losing all control of her bodily functions, she rolled on the ground pulling her hair, beating herself with her fists.

Women ran from the train to bring her back.

"Let me die. Oh, please let me die," she moaned to them. "I don't want to live any longer."

The women had to drag her back by her arms as Doris refused to stand or crawl.

Shepherd stood with open mouth until the women dragged Mrs. Hopkins to the confines of the wagons. Turning to the Yoncallas, as they crept out of hiding, he wasn't sure if he should pull his gun and run or act like the hysterical sight that just played out never happened.

Quinn stepped up next to him, watching to see what the Yoncallas might do.

"Now what?" Shepherd said low under his breath. He watched every movement made as the Indians brushed off their leggings and tried to regain some decorum.

"Keep close together. Keep your gun in your belt until we see what they think of what just happened. Injuns is peculiar sometimes." He reached over and brushed some pine straw off a chief's shoulder. The chief looked grimly at Quinn.

Quinn tried to explain that the woman's husband had been killed and that he was the one who shot the young brave by mistake. He offered the milk cow, holding the heifer in reserve if he needed to add more to the pot. A deal was made to return the woman the Indians had taken. Quinn lied when he told the chief she was a sister to Mrs. Hopkins, and once she found out about Reverend Hopkins dying, he would have to face another crazy woman.

The chief spoke low and deliberately. He told Quinn about the many mishaps lately with the pilgrims. He wanted the whites to go away.

Quinn watched the chief's face as he continued his long

monologue.

Shepherd whispered in Quinn's ear. "What's he saying?"

"They're tired of the whites running off the game and killing their braves. He will take the milk cow since the man who murdered the young brave is dead. It is something. They have lost too many men. Their women cry at night. He wants to be left in peace and the whites to be gone. The Hopkins woman has spooked them. They feel she has been teched by spirits, and the sooner they get out of here, the better they will like it. They are returning the other woman, pronto. They don't want a crazy white woman stirring up the evil spirits. He has enough to worry about."

"I feel the same way," Shepherd said over his shoulder.

"Damn crazy white women." The chief made a cutting motion, indicating he was through and stood back waiting.

"Go get the milk cow from Brother Morse, and let's get this over with," Quinn urged Shepherd to skedaddle and bring back the cow.

When Shepherd motioned for Morse to bring the cow to him, Jon relaxed little.

"Damn fine cow. She made it the entire journey here, raised her calf along the way. I'll miss her. Funny…my cow, The Reverend, and Mrs. Hopkins ended their lives on the same day. Hard to figure how things work out sometimes." Brother Morse sat next to Jon with his head in his hands. "Think the Injuns will leave and not come back?"

"I think they've had enough. Are you're going to Salem?"

"We are."

"We've got a couple of good bulls at our ranch. You can breed your heifer to one of them when she is ready. Help ya get some stock for your place, wherever you go."

"That's a kind offer, stranger. I'll do just that."

A subdued group sat around the fire that night. They had buried their leader along with the others who had been killed. Doris Hopkins was wrapped in blankets after the women had cleaned her up. She refused to wear clothes. They had to bind her hands and tie her in her wagon so she wouldn't hurt herself or run away.

Quinn, Jon, and Shepherd guiltily enjoyed the bacon and biscuits they dined on that evening. Quinn even finagled a chaw, but he wouldn't tell anyone where he got it.

Quinn volunteered to lead the wagons into the Willamette Valley and up to Oregon City for an agreed-upon price.

Shepherd was to take his prisoner on in ahead of them. At least, that was how it felt to Jon. His fate awaited him, and he dreaded what lay ahead. The next few days, before he got into town, were the longest of his life.

CHAPTER 23

———— ◆◇◆ ————

Quinn took charge immediately. The dead had been buried and prayers said over them. Eleanor Branch, the returned woman, was unharmed except for a few scrapes and bruises and the scare of her life. He saw that the group was separated into two divisions of three wagons each, and he appointed two men as division supervisors with instructions to report to him.

"Who's the man who's been shooting the shotgun? I want that shotgun up front when we leave here. The Indians have seen it and will respect it."

A short man wearing pants and a wool flannel shirt rolled up to his elbows stepped forward. He held the shotgun across his body. His floppy brimmed hat hid his features. "I ain't a givin' up ma shotgun to nobody. It was my pa's, and he left it to me."

"Huh. Let me see your face. I wanta know who I'm a talkin' to at least." Quinn stood back studying the short man.

"I ain't no man. I ain't no girl, neither, mister." A blonde woman shook out her hair from underneath the large hat and looked Quinn defiantly in the eye. "I ain't a givin' ya ma gun!"

"Ya don't need to, ma'am, if you can shoot that thing as

good as you did. You got a wagon?"

"I do."

"You got a man?"

"I don't. He got hisself killed back a ways." She lifted her chin. "I've handled everything just fine, by the way. I can work as good as anyone else here."

Brother Morse broke the silence. "She has done a good job. An asset to the train. I can vouch for her, even if she is a woman." Several of the men and women nodded in assent.

"Didn't mean any disrespect, ma'am. What's your name?"

"Married name is Faith Anne Marshall. What's yours?"

"Everybody calls me Quinn, ma'am."

"Pleased ta meet cha, Mr. Quinn." She gestured to the side. "What do you want me to do?"

"I want your wagon to lead this train. I'm going to ride with you, and I want that shotgun close at hand all the time." He lowered his chin a notch. "Can you do that?"

"I can." Confidence rang in those two words.

"Any objections to Mrs. Marshall's wagon leading the way?" Quinn asked the men folk. No one objected. "All right, then. Let's move these wagons. Make way thar. Let Mrs. Marshall's wagon through, and let's move away from here before them Indians change their mind."

Six wagons rolled away from that place of death. Quinn drove from up on the seat, his horse tied behind the wagon. Faith Anne Marshall sat next to him with her daddy's double-barreled shotgun gripped in both hands.

Watchful eyes studied the close, verdant forest, looking for unknown dangers. Limbs brushed dirty white canvas as they passed. Wagons lumbered over old growth roots and ancient rocks, bumping and lurching into the soft fingers of pine, spruce, and fir. The trail gave way to groves of birch and aspen.

A cacophony of voices echoed, "Git up there! Move up,

Blue. Come on, Jenny and Jake!" Calls and whistles bounced back and forth across the boulders and forest canopy as the train sprung to life, moving forward on their never-ending trek north to new land and hard-won freedom.

Mrs. Hopkins huddled in thick blankets, red-eyed, horrified, looking out the rear flap of her wagon on a foreign landscape. A place feared and hated. The dark forest's fingers beckoned her back, alluringly evil, calling to her, waving to her, pointing at her. The white birch cross marker over her husband's grave was the last sane moment she remembered.

"How ya feeling about all of this?" Shepherd glanced at Jon. "I know it's weighing on your mind. You haven't spoken a word in two days. You still gonna go do this?"

The two rode abreast on the trail to Salem. The Willamette River flowed to the north on their left. They were following the old Siskiyou trail, sometimes wandering close to the river and, often as not, away from the river straightening their route. Shepherd figured they had about three days of travel time to Salem.

"It's alright. I'm going through with it." Jon shook his head. "Don't figure I have ever been in such a predicament before. Feeling I was doing the right thing by avenging our pa. Getting rid of evil men, who would continue being evil, because they was no one else to stop them. Now, the law wants *me* to be accountable when Whitey and his gang *weren't* held accountable. We'll see how it goes. I want to stop at the ranch before I turn myself in. Okay with you?"

Shepherd nodded.

Cold rain started up slowly, building to a steady

downpour by midafternoon. That evening, they sat around a smoky fire, huddled under a canvas lean-to for cover.

"Hope this stops soon." Jon tried to scoot deeper beneath the canvas. Little good it did. "I'm wet and getting wetter. Our wood isn't going to last till morning."

"There's some coffee left in the pot. We'll have some cold coffee, at least to get us started on the trail." Shepherd gave a rough chuckle. "Gonna be a miserable night, I grant you that."

"Hello, the fire! Can we come in?" voices called from the sodden blackness.

Horses snorted and stomped their feet beyond the feeble firelight.

"Who's there?" Shepherd asked.

Jon slipped behind the lean-to, rifle in hand.

"Name's Sweet. Evan Sweet. I got three other fellas with me. We're headed home from Salem. Mind if we share your fire?"

"It ain't much, but you're welcome. Come in single file. Hands out and open. Leave your hardware on your mounts."

One by one, four men exited the shadows, holding out their hands, rain dripping off their hats and clothes. They each stepped before the fire, lifting their slickers so Shepherd could see they had no guns.

"Name?"

"Neal Smith." A kid of sixteen or so announced, his hands empty.

"Jack Bitterman," said another, as he lifted the skirts of his poncho.

"They call me Indian Joe." Man, number three raised the wide brim edge of his hat, revealing a dark face with a long scar down the left side. He wore no poncho.

A large man stepped to the edge of the fire, raising his poncho revealing no guns. "I'm Sweet. Call off your man, will you? We introduced ourselves. We're harmless."

Jon stepped around the side of the lean-to, rifle held at ready.

"They just seem wet and cold like us." Shepherd motioned for him to lower his gun.

Jon sat next to Shepherd and threw another branch onto the fire. "We ain't got much more wood, fellas, but you're welcome to the camp. Go ahead and bring your horses round and get yourselves set up."

Opposite them, the men erected a similar lean-to similar by the fire. They saw to their horses, leaving them with feed bags over their noses, before settling underneath the poor shelter their canvas offered.

Jon poked around and brought in another armful of wet wood, dropping it close to the fire to dry. "Nice to have a bit of company. We're headed to Salem ourselves." He sat next to Shepherd then rubbed his hands together over the fire.

Jack Bitterman pulled out some jerky from his bedroll. "Jerky?"

"Don't mind if I do." Jon rose and took several long black sticks of jerky. He passed a couple to Shepherd who nodded his thanks to Bitterman.

"'Fraid all we got to offer you boys is some leftover coffee, but you're welcome to it." Shepherd set the pot closer to the fire.

"Even warmed-up coffee is welcome in this weather." Evan Sweet dug a tin cup out of his possibles bag and set it next to the coal to warm up while he waited for the coffee to heat. The other three men did the same, rubbing their hands over the fire then sitting back, shrugging deeper into their clothes, as their travel-worn faces stared into the flames.

"At least we're out of the rain." Neal leaned over and helped himself to the jerky in Bitterman's leather pouch.

"There is that," Sweet replied.

The men sat musing their own thoughts, sipping coffee,

and gnawing on jerky sticks as they listened to the rain pit-a-pat on the canvas and leaves, dripping into the duff of the forest floor.

"Don't believe I caught you boys' names?" Sweet broke the dark silence. "Like to know who I'm sharin' camp with."

"Oh, sorry. I'm Shepherd McKinzey, and this is my brother, Jon. We got a ranch south of Salem."

Sweet looked up and then over to Indian Joe, his demeanor calm, his eyes hardened.

"I think I'll see if I can find some more wood." Joe stood up and stretched. "Indians gotta be better at finding wood than white men or black men. Ned, come help. I'll show you how to find dry wood in the rain." They shuffled through the wet leaves off toward the horses.

Sweet smiled at Shepherd. "Joe's making a joke. No offense meant."

"None taken," replied Shepherd. "He's probably right."

"Seems I've heard of you boys back in town. Been on the trail long?"

Alarm crept up Shepherd's spine, but he kept his nervousness to himself. "Awhile. How about you boys? Where's home?"

"Gold City."

Both Jon and Shepherd stood up.

"We've been looking for you, Jon McKinzey. You killed friends of ours."

Jon pointed his rifle at Sweet's face. "Men who killed my pa, Sweet, and burned down my ranch."

"Funny, that's what happened to me, too." He nodded at the men who had crept up behind Shepherd and Jon.

Explosions erupted in both Jon's and Shepherd's heads, dropping them as rifle butts cracked against their skulls. Indian Joe and Ned immediately bound their hands and legs.

Indian Joe pressed a knife to Jon's neck.

"Wait, Joe. Don't kill them yet. We'll hang Jon and make his black brother watch. Leave them where they lay for now. We'll do it in the morning. I'll take first watch. Get some sleep."

Jon woke to a kick in his back. Bright sunshine blinded him, and his body ached in every joint and fiber of his being from cold and stiffness. Not even being shot had hurt so much.

"Sweet. He's awake." Jack Bitterman stepped back and jabbed Jon with his rifle butt again.

"Get him up. Get the other one up, too. I want to hear what they got to say before I hang 'em."

Shepherd stood up stiffly, glaring at Sweet. "Think before you go ahead with any of this. My badge is in my possibles bag. I'm a sworn deputy marshal of this territory. I'm bringing Jon back for trial. If you kill us, the entire territory will be searching for you."

"I didn't see any shackles or ropes being used. Didn't look like no prisoner I ever seen." Sweet sipped a bit of his coffee. "We heard you was his brother from people in the town."

"Told you last night we was going in to Salem. I'm turning myself in." Jon held his hands up. "Cut me loose. That's why we're here. I'm going to stand trial. You can say your piece there. At least cut Shepherd loose. He ain't done nothin' to you. All that was done was done by me. Nobody else."

Sweet waved his hand to Indian Joe to cut Shepherd's bonds.

Joe protested, "We gots to kill these boys, or they'll come after us. You know that, Sweet."

"I'm boss here, Indian Joe, but you do got a point, so leave him be. We got to act like law-abiding citizens. I want him to watch. He'll swing next."

"You are interfering in my duties as deputy marshal. You'll let us go our own way, or I'll file a report with all of your names."

"That may be, Mr. Deputy, but you see, your brother Jon, here, killed some friends of ours."

"Which one of the scum I killed was your friend?" Jon snarled.

"Hilton was his name," Jack snapped at him.

"He's Jack's brother. Thanks for getting rid of Whitey, by the way. He was becoming too big a man in town. Started crowding me out." Sweet smiled at the thought.

"Hilton had no call to be in the fight. I came for Whitey and his gang. Your friend should a kept out of it."

Jack hit Jon between the shoulder blades with the butt of his rifle, dropping him to his knees. "He was my brother, Hilton Bitterman. You say his name with respect, or I'll blow you to kingdom come right here and now." He raised his rifle to Jon's face.

"Stop it, Jack. I've heard enough. Let's get this done and over with. Get him up on a horse. I'm tired. We all want to get back home. Lucky, we ran into y'all like we did. Didn't think they was gonna ta do anything back in the town with our complaint anyways. This wraps up everything nice and tidy."

"'Cept what you going to do with me? Deputy marshals don't just disappear without an investigation, ya know. They'll find out about what happened here. Think on that, big man."

"I have, Mr. Deputy. There's no law in Injun lands. There will be no witnesses. None of us knew what happened. We never saw you boys at all. We came down on the other side of the river. Saw nobody. Got any more opinions?" Sweet sneered. "Get McKinzey on a horse. Daylight is wastin'." He surveyed the forest for a hanging tree. He pointed to it. "There's one over there. Let's go! Jack, get his horse."

Jack sprinted for the picket line.

Only Shepherd saw the raven fly to the top of the

hanging tree. He screeched once then began preening his feathers.

Jack's yell startled everyone. He came limping back, cussing under his breath, rubbing his arm and his leg.

"What's wrong with you? That's my horse." Sweet stared at Jack as if he were deaf.

"If you want that black devil, you go get him. He bit me and kicked me when I tried to untie him. Your horse will have to do." Jack pulled the horse over by Jon and stood rubbing his arm with one hand and rubbing his leg with the other foot.

"Get on with it, then," Sweet demanded.

Jack and Neal hauled Jon up onto Sweet's horse and led them to the tree Evan had pointed to. Indian Joe placed a loop around Jon's neck, smirking as he did it, snugging the noose and jerking it a few times until Jon's face turned purple, the veins in his neck swelling.

Shepherd pleaded, "I never wanted to see a hanging rope ever again. God, please don't do this!"

A wagon's chains rattled over a bump in the thick of the forest. "Move up there, mule." More calls were heard behind the wall of thick forest, hiding the approaching wagons. Shepherd and Jon looked at each other as several wagons crept out of the forest following the way north.

Quinn glanced over at the group of men, seeing Jon tied on a horse sitting under a tree, a rope around his neck. One of them held the other end of the rope. Shepherd's hands were tied. Quinn spat over the side of the wagon, nodded, and kept driving until he was right next to the tree himself.

He said in a low voice so no one else could hear, "Faith Anne, why don't you aim that scattergun you got over on the man with the rope in his hands. Don't shoot lessen's I say, or if somebody shoots me."

In a louder voice he said, "What goes on here, boys? Looks like you're about ta hang this man. We got women and children in these wagons. Salem ain't so far a ways that you couldn't take him there for his wrong doin'. What did he do?"

Faith Anne rested the barrel of her gun on the side of her wagon, pointed at Indian Joe's chest.

"Keep on travelin', pilgrim. This ain't no concern of yours. We'll wait till you pass, to spare the women and children. Keep moving." Sweet walked over to grab the mule's bridles to lead him on.

Quinn stood up. "Don't touch ma mule."

Indian Joe threw down the rope, grabbed the knife at his belt, and drew back to throw it.

Faith Anne pulled both triggers on her daddy's double-barreled shotgun, blasting pieces of Joe up a tall pine tree.

At Faith Anne's blast, Jon's horse reared, throwing him off onto the duff of the forest floor. He lay stunned for a brief moment, the rope curling down over his face from the branch above. Coming to his senses, he shook off the rope and wiggled his way behind his hanging tree, getting out of the line of fire.

Sweet drew his gun and fired at Quinn. Quinn ducked and fired back, hitting Sweet in the right shoulder. Sweet fell under the mules. Excited and scared by the gunfire, the mules lurched forward, pulling the wagon over Evan Sweet.

Shepherd dashed to the lean-to and grabbed his pistol. "Damn these ropes!" He managed firing over the top of Neal and Jack's heads, stopping them in their tracks before they could draw their guns. "Stay right where you are, or you'll join your friends."

"Whoa, mule! Whoa." Quinn pulled the reins, getting the mules under control. He leaped over the side to check on Sweet, but he came up shaking his head. "Nothing ta be done for him. He's had it. What in tarnation is going on here?" He looked at Shepherd.

"We got waylaid by Mr. Evan Sweet and his boys. You two." He motioned to Neal and Jack. "Cut Jonny loose and take that goddamn noose off his neck, or I'll have this pretty little lady blow you away like Injun Joe and run the damn mules over you, crushing you into the mud like Sweet."

Neal and Jack just stood there. Shepherd fired a shot at their feet. "Move! My patience is wearing mighty thin with you two boys."

"That's Sweet under the wagon. Those are pieces of Indian Joe scattered up that pine tree and these two remaining gents is Jack Bitterman and young Neal Smith. They're from Gold City. Seems they all had a grudge against Jon and meant to do something about some friends of theirs he might have killed."

Jon shook his hands free and rubbed them until they came back to life. His right cross caught Jack Bitterman full flush on the chin. The man fell like a stuck pig. "That's for this morning." He looked at Neal. "You the one who cold cocked me last night?"

Neal sprinted to Shepherd and tried to hide behind him.

"Don't hide behind me, boy. I should give you one myself." Shepherd turned and kicked him in his privates.

A deep "oomff" came from Neal's mouth, who danced away, grabbed his crotch, and slipped into a deep muddy hole up to his chest, white-faced and gasping for breath.

"Sorry, Mister Quinn. You told me to wait to shoot, but I couldn't let him stick you with his knife. I had ta shoot." Faith Anne jumped off the wagon and hurried to Quinn's side.

"You did right fine, Faith Anne. I owe you. Ya did right. It's an honor to ride with someone who's lookin' out for me."

Shepherd glanced at Jon, nodding his head toward Quinn.

Jon smirked, but then a movement up in the treetops drew his eye. A raven flew toward Salem.

CHAPTER 24

Quinn led the wagons into town while Shepherd and Jon parted with them at the ranch.

"Tell Lyle we'll be into town once we get business here squared away," Jon told Quinn. "A couple more days won't make no difference to anyone, I don't suppose."

Jon and Shepherd paused before the charred gate leading to the ranch. "I know this don't seem like home to you yet. Mac and me had big plans for after you got here." Shepherd led the way toward where the ranch house had stood.

They stopped at their father's grave site, and both dismounted.

After a few minutes, Shepherd put his arm around his brother. "It's just us now, Jonny."

"Is that why you're bringing me back, Shepherd?"

"Damn right it is. You need to get this thing behind you. Being a wanted man don't add up to no good for you or me. If you killed a deputy or got killed, I'd never forget it. Either way, I lose you."

"What do you mean?"

"I take no pleasure in bringing you in for trial. Those men deserved what they got. I wish I had more to do with their deaths. However, as it stands, this may work out for both of us. I know we both want to go back to ranchin'. Once this is done we can do that…otherwise."

"Otherwise?" Jon squatted in the grass next to Mac's gravestone.

"Otherwise, my brother, I promise you this. If you are found guilty, I'll break you out of there if I have to kill every son-of-a-bitch in the town. We'll go outlaw. I will have nothing to do with putting a rope around your neck. You will not hang if I have a drop of blood left in me."

Jon looked up at his brother. "You'd do that?"

"I would." He gave a hard nod. "On the other hand, we have property here. Mac filed on all of our names. This ranch is close to five hundred acres. We can have the life we dreamed of once this business is behind us. We got to take care of how we go about it. I got some ideas I will take up with Lyle." He turned and walked toward the horses. "C'mon. Let me show you around."

They mounted.

"The house was big." Shepherd's voice was proud but held a note of sadness, too. "Four bedrooms upstairs. Two downstairs. Mac said he wanted to hear little steps running all over the house when we had babies, so he built it big. The barns and corrals are all still standing. The horses we brought back are all out to pasture. Quinn and I released them on plenty of grass. Lyle said he'd ride out and look after them until we come in."

They rode through rich green pastures and towering virgin forests, splashed across cold bubbling streams, and breathed in the fragrance that was their home place. They topped a low rise, viewing a large lake on the downhill side.

"Lake is full of trout," Shepherd mused. "Mac and I built a stone hunting dugout down there. It's a rich land. Mac saw it when we first explored the place. We had a start on raising horses. Derry was to be our resident stud, building our own breed over the years. Our mares have all been bred to him. They'll be foaling next spring. We were just waiting for you, for us to bust out in the horse business, when Whitey and his gang showed up." Shepherd stood up in his stirrups, looking around. "I owe it to you and Mac to see that it will happen. We have to live on it for five years and it is ours. Mac and I have been here just two years, goin' on three. If we leave, the place goes back to the state. That's another reason we have to win. Plus, I haven't seen your skinny butt breaking broncs for two years. You still any good?"

"I'm better. I didn't just dry up back in Indianapolis. I still broke stock and sold them until we got our stake. The ranch went for top dollar when I sold it. We've got a lot of money in the bank in Salem."

They grew quiet as they scanned the verdant hills and forests. Their land—fought, died, and killed for. They rode on, coming full circle to where they'd started.

Jon surveyed the charred remains of what their father had built. "Should we build the house where it stood, or should we move it?"

"We'll build, right where it stood. It'll feel like Mac is still with us in a way." Shepherd glanced around then gave a deep sigh. "Ready?"

"You know what?" Jon looked toward his father's grave then back to the beauty surrounding them. *Home, finally.* "I am ready. You've brought everything into perspective. Let's get this over with. We got a lot to do. Race you to the gate." Jon whistled to Derry, and the horse took off like a shot.

Shepherd's horse reared in surprise. "Whoa, Sandy." He calmed his mount then whistled his own shrill sound. "Go get them!" He kicked Sandy in the flanks, and the race was on.

Lyle Newton was entering the lane, when the yipping and whistles caught his ear. He pulled up to see what the racket was about. The two brothers raced toward him, going hell for leather and bragging rights.

Jon pulled up first. When his gaze fell on Lyle, his face took on a serious demeaner from the spirited enthusiasm he had previously.

Shepherd slid to a halt, but Sandy pranced around, fighting the bit. "What's the matter, Lyle? Didn't Quinn tell you we were coming in?"

"They did all right. Quinn told me the whole story, about them wagons you all saved and about that hanging. Glad you came out of that, too. Trouble is, it just makes Jon's story bigger and bigger. That's why I came out. I'd like to escort Jon into town. No telling what folks might do. There's a great deal of talk in town about your brother. Some think he should hang. Others think he did the right thing in ridding the world of those wolves."

"What side are you on, Lyle?" Shepherd's question was direct.

"Hell, boys. If I could, I'd pin a medal in his shirt. He saved me and the territory a lot of time and trouble. Our problem, Deputy McKinzey, is we're the law, and we have a job to do. I hope we have an understanding amongst us?"

Shepherd nodded.

"Jon, I'll do my best for you, but we got to take you in. There's evidence on both sides. I hope a fair-minded jury sees it your way."

"I'm ready, Marshal. That's where Shep and I were headed after I beat his pants off on Derry."

"We were heading into town, Lyle. That is the truth. My hand on it." Shepherd rode next to Lyle, offering his hand.

Lyle took it. "Never thought any different. Let's ride."

The three men rode down the road abreast of each other.

Lyle cleared his throat. "Jon, I hesitate to bring it up, but as we get close to town, I'm going to put you in shackles. It'll be safer for you and keep speculating talk down around town."

"I didn't consider that, Marshal, but I understand. I

won't like it, but I understand. Just so you know, however, I won't be manhandled by anyone outside of this group. I will give back more than what was given." Jon rode ahead.

Shepherd rode next to Lyle. "I have an idea if we can get some deputies to carry it out."

Lyle listened closely, nodding. "I'll see to that as soon as we're in town. Anything I can do to help, let me know. Mac was a good friend to me and a lot of folks in town. He was well thought of."

CHAPTER 25

J on recognized the mission school and hospital as they neared town. He took a deep breath as memories of his reunion with Shepherd flooded back.

"This is a good time." Lyle dismounted and went to his saddlebags. He pulled a pair of manacles out of the left side then approached Jon with an apologetic grimace on his face.

"No! Stop. I'll do it. The clanging of those things sends chills up my back. I've hated those damn things my whole life. I'll not see them on Jonny." Shepherd dropped off his horse and pulled some rawhide out of his packs. "This'll work just as well." He lashed Jon's hands together loosely and passed a few loops over his saddle horn to make it appear secure. "That should pass. Don't you think?"

Lyle replaced the manacles. "It'll do. We ain't undergoing no close inspections, I suspect. Jon, you got to promise me to behave once we get into town. Some pernicious upstart likely will be feelin' his oats and try to start somethin', seeing you all bound up. Shep, wear your badge outside your coat, so's it can be seen. Once we get to the jail, just keep your mouth shut and we'll handle any Jake that tries for you." His eyes turned toward Jon.

"I'll go along, Lyle, but I won't tolerate being handled,

like I said. Let's get this over with." Clucking to Derry, he led the way down the road.

Lyle and Shepherd had to hurry to catch up. Lyle grabbed Derry's reins, taking the lead. Shepherd guarded their rear as they entered Salem.

Bystanders stopped on the raised sidewalks, staring at the men as they moved down the street. Dogs nipped at the heels of the horses. Pigs moved out of the mud and sought refuge under the boardwalks as the lonesome trio made its way to the jail. Lyle wanted the town to see Jon McKinzey was in custody. They stopped in front of the jail.

Lyle pulled out his coach gun from a boot on the right side of his saddle. He slid off his horse with a warning on his face. "We got Jonny McKinzey. I tol' Judge Blakely I was going after him. Trial starts next Monday morning." He climbed the steps to the boardwalk in front of the door to the jail. "Bring him in, Shep."

"Is that the horse thief and killer I've heard so much about? He's only a boy." A woman stepped forward behind Marshal Newton to get a better view. "I thought he'd be much older."

"He's old enough, Maddie. Now give way there. I want some room on this walkway." The marshal turned to the crowd forming on his right and left, moving them back with his menacing scowl. "Get him down."

Shepherd loosened Jon's bonds from the saddle horn so he could dismount, stepping back to allow his brother room to slide onto the street.

"Sooo, that's McKinzey!" A pale man dressed neatly in a black shirt and pants leaned against a post on the sidewalk. "He killed my brother out by Wolf Springs, ya know. He is just a kid! A killer kid!" His black hat hid his face, but his voice was loud, fueled by whiskey trader drink and false confidence. "Let's see if he's man enough to hang. I want to see this face. His yellow killer kid face." As he stepped down the steps, he removed his hat, revealing displaced eyes that seemed to look at opposite sides of the street at the same time.

Shepherd nodded toward the man. Holding Jon's arm, he guided him toward the steps Lyle was on. "Go on, Jonny. I'll handle this."

＊-◦✤◦-＊

His hands still bound together, Jon shook his head in disgust. He watched the man on the street as he climbed the steps to stand beside Lyle.

"Go back to your drinking, friend. We've got this well in order. You can see him at the trial." Shepherd held up his hand to stop the oncoming man in black.

"What's this? The darky brother? A deputy? The darky brother is his deputy! A darky deputy! Now ain't that a whale of a lot of horse shit. Sounds like cooo-llusion to me. Are all of ya blind?" He turned around, appealing to the crowded streets. "Are you going to let this happen in our city? What's he got in his saddlebags? What does a killer kid bring wiff him?" He dumped Jon's saddlebags onto the street. "What the hell is this?"

He held up the shirt Laughing Grass had made for Jon after the peyote healing. It was a beaded raven in full flight on the front of the buck skin. His feathered headband fell out as well. "We got ourselves a damn Injun lover. No wonder that kid's a killer. A damn killer redskin lover is what he is." Holding the shirt up, he paraded the shirt and headdress around the street.

Alarmed at all the chatter he'd caused, Lyle called out, "Now wait a minute. The man is going to trial. His brother brought him in peaceable, like he was deputized to do. No call for more trouble. Go home to your wives and families.

175

I've got this in hand." He directed a look, that was meant to freeze anyone in their tracks, at the man in black. "Mister, get off my street. What's your name?"

"I'm Jonah Smith." He threw Jon's belongings into the street. Arrogance emanated from his bearing. Both thumbs hooked in his gun belt, he stood bandy-legged, one foot stamping Jon's shirt into the mud, a taunting smile on his face.

"Well, Mr. Smith, say your piece at the trial. Now shut the hell up, and go home!"

"You can't tell me what to do, Marshal. I'm a tax-paying citizen." He grinned, pushing his hat back on his head. "I want to stare that Indian-loving, killer kid in the face." He started forward.

"Go ahead, Shepherd." Lyle's voice was sharp and clear.

Shepherd's fist met Jonah's face in mid step, knocking his hat into the street. His eyes crossed, and he sagged a little. Shepherd pulled him up by his shirt front. "You was told to get gone." Shep pushed him toward the other side of the street. "Stay gone."

Unsteadily, the man retrieved his hat, holding up his hand to Shepherd and nodding in a pleading manner. After pulling it in place, he waited until Shepherd turned his back.

Shepherd heard the crowd gasp then the click of the hammer. He ducked in time, the shot flying over his head and striking a donkey tied to a hitching post.

The donkey brayed and kicked furiously as blood spurted from its flank. The donkey fell into the mud, kicking and screaming, reins wrapped around its neck. It died in a twisted convoluted position strangling on the reins. Its lifeblood pulsed from its body in an ever-weakening, oozing stream.

Time seemed to slow to a muted, measured crawl for Shepherd as he saw all of this and centered his attention on the smirking man holding the smoking gun. Rage propelled him forward, but he felt himself moving as if encased in clear thick goo, vision fuzzy, hearing skewed.

On his third step, he caught up to present time, as if he'd stepped back into it from another dimension, and crashed into Jonah Smith, folding the man in half like a bent stick. Colors and sounds returned so vivid, they shocked his senses like sudden lightning.

Jonah's hat flew forward, his face shocked from the blow, turned whiter, his eyes bulged from their sockets. The smoking gun flew over Shepherd's back.

Pain shot through his hand as he smashed Jonah's mouth, breaking the front teeth, blooding his face and nose. Sitting astride the fallen man, his weight bearing him into the muddy street, he struck the taunting face again and again, bruising flesh, blacking eyes, and breaking bones. Enjoying the satisfaction of crushing that face into bloody pulp, Shepherd raised back to land a thunderous left, but Lyle caught his fist.

"He's had enough, man. Let him go." Lyle held on to Shep's arm until the madness faded from the deputy's face. "Get up, Mr. Smith. You're under arrest for attempted murder of a U.S. Deputy Marshal."

Fear replaced the arrogance in Jonah's eyes. Fear of impending doom. He crawled up to his feet, dabbing the blood from his face with the mud-stained sleeve of his white shirt. "I won't forget this, Marshal." He could barely mumble, his jaw broke in two places, he dribbled broken bits of teeth into the street. Blowing bloody snot through his nose onto the blood-stained sleeve, he winced and struggled to take a deep breath.

"You'd better. Next time, I'll let Shepherd finish the job and save the territory the cost of hanging you." Grabbing the man's arm, he pulled him toward the jail. He waved for the brothers to go in.

Grim determination etched Lyle's face as he turned to the crowd and fired one barrel of his shotgun into the air.

"Go home," he shouted. "We won't be trifled with. Someone, send Dr. Chalmers to patch this man up. I'm holding him for attempted murder." He pushed Jonah through the door and turned to follow.

Seeing Maddie still on the boardwalk, he called out to her, "Would you please have your husband, Royce, come pay us a call? I think I have some business for him."

"It's for the boy, isn't it? Of course. I understand. I'll go right away."

CHAPTER 26

Royce Stuart stomped off the mud from the street on the first step. Then he climbed up to the boardwalk. He stood over six feet tall with a shock of long white hair, wearing a black frock coat and pants, black riding boots, and a white starched collar. "Confounded mud," he said under his breath. He beat at the dried mud on his trousers with a black journal he held. When he'd finished, he pulled a handkerchief from his coat pocket and wiped the journal clean.

After a deep sigh, he walked up to the marshal's office, using an ivory-headed black cane to punctuate each step. This was more than a status symbol. He had carried some form of cane since leaving the old country. Here, there was no blackthorn, like he had carried in Scotland to fight off thieves and usurpers. So far, this black substitute had sufficed.

He wasn't looking forward to this summons. Lyle and he were old friends. From what Maddie described to him of this morning's events, he wasn't sure what his old friend was going to ask. It did not bode well in his mind. Not at all. He knocked briskly.

A view port slid back on the door. "Who's calling? State your business."

"It's Royce Stuart. Marshal Newton asked to see me." Royce moved so his face could be seen.

"Marshal, a Mr. Stuart is here for you," a man hollered to the back of the jail.

"Let him come in, Shep. I sent for him." Lyle's voice offered Royce a little assurance.

Shepherd opened the door, gave Royce the once-over then suspiciously looked up and down the street. It seemed the man sniffing the air as well as checking for anyone lurking about.

"Come in, Royce. Have a seat." Lyle walked into the front room of the jail, wiping his hands on a clean towel. "Want a drink? I got some of that good Scotch whisky, you gave me last week."

"I am a Scot. You know that is a stupid question. I don't drink when I work. Luckily, I'm not in the courtroom today. I will have just a wee dram. Then let's talk business. Maddie has been driving me crazy until I took leave of her to come for your summons. She was saying something about an Indian boy who was a child killer?"

"Something like that. Here's your drink. What did you tell me about the Scottish toast? Oh, I think I remember. *Slainte ma hath!* Health! Is that correct?"

"Very good, Lyle, and I respond, *Do dheagh shlainte.* To your good health! I'll make a Scot out of ye yet!" Royce sat down, sniffed his glass, showed his approval, sipped, sipped again then swished the drink in his mouth and swallowed, smacking his lips with gusto.

"Now, what is this all about?" He crossed his legs and lounged back into the chair, one hand supported by the black cane at his side, his eyes fixed on Lyle.

"Shepherd, do you drink Scotch? This is a fine example of it." Lyle proffered a glass toward his deputy, who shrugged a no.

"Maybe another time, Marshal. I'll stay on watch."

Lyle rubbed his chin, pursed his lips then pulled a chair

to sit in front of Royce. "You're the best attorney in town, Royce. Probably the best in the territory. You practiced law in the old country and were a well-known attorney until the trouble started.

"Yes, yes. I was a reputable solicitor. Old family names still fighting each other, despite millennia of time passing, caught up to me. You know I was run out by the damn English. They almost killed my entire family. Fortunately, most of us got away." He flicked his fingers, encouraging Lyle to continue. "Forget all that. What is it I can do for you?"

"Shepherd's brother here, Jon McKinzey, is going to be placed on trial for murder. I'd like you to represent him."

He raised a brow. "Did he do the deed?"

"Yes, he did. There were plenty of witnesses to the killings."

Royce leaned forward, supporting his hands on his cane. "Go ahead."

Shep interrupted, "Our pa, John McKinzey, was killed by these men. I was shot up. Our home burned to the ground. Stock was run off or stolen. The men who done it. They was from an old feud, started clear back in Indianapolis, when we were boys. It was a revenge killing, deliberate and planned. Jonny hunted them down and killed them, that was part of it."

"Wait, I met a John McKinzey a few years ago. He was a white man as I remember. Is this the killing of the same man you told me about several months ago, Lyle? No one went after them? I remember some of what you told me." Royce sat up straight, his eyes shiny and alert. "Can I talk to your Jonny?"

Lyle opened the door to the back part of the jail. "Jon, come in here, will you. I want you to meet Royce Stuart."

Jon wore a serious look when he walked into the room.

Royce was visibly taken aback that Jon was white.

Lyle smiled a little. "Yeah, he's a surprise after meeting

Shepherd, isn't he?"

"I was adopted by the McKinzey's when I was a young boy," Shepherd said.

"That clears that up, I suppose." Royce stood. "Royce Stuart, Mr. Jon McKinzey."

"Glad to meet you, sir," Jon said.

They clasped hands.

"You are very young." Royce walked around Jon, taking his measure. "The McKinzeys and the Stuarts used to be closely linked during the monarchy, though everything was spelled differently back in the old country. Did you know that? I see the fighting spirit hasn't been dimmed by generations. There is little trace of The Highlands in your speech."

"We've had three generations in this country now, sir. Besides, I got tired of fighting every boy who made fun of any accent I had left when I was in school."

"Hmm." Royce rubbed his chin. "You killed...how many?"

"He killed eight," Lyle supplied. "Face-to-face, mainly."

"There were also the two that tried to hang us," Shepherd added. "But Jonny did not kill them."

"Fascinating. McKinzeys always were fighters. I admire that." Royce looked Jon up and down. "You don't seem to have a mark on you."

Jon pulled up his shirt to reveal his scars. "Got raked by a shotgun at the end of it. I was fixed up by my brother and my friend Quinn Taylor. But mainly, I was healed by Flying Eagle, a Shoshone shaman, in a peyote healing ceremony."

"Eight men? Lyle, before I commit to this, I would like to talk to Jon. Do you have a room where he and I can talk privately? I could also interview him at my office, if that is acceptable."

"No, we'll do it here. Shep, take them to that empty cell next to Jon's. The cells are empty, now that Jonah Smith is over in the infirmary, being treated by Dr. Chalmers. I can't let him out of this office, Royce. Too many folks want him dead. Make sure you close the door for privacy. I don't want anyone to suspect we're playing sides here. Take all the time you need, Royce. I want him to have a fair trial."

For the better part of two hours, Lyle and Shepherd paced, peeked out the window, drank stale coffee, and read and reread newspapers and the few magazines they had in the office. Both were as nervous as they could be. They jumped when loud boot steps sounded outside the door, paused, and moved on. Sheepishly, they smiled at each other at their tenseness.

"What is taking so damn long?" Shepherd threw a well-worn magazine to the floor. "I'll take a taste of that whiskey now if you don't mind, Marshal. I am as jumpy as a bedbug. Maybe it will calm my nerves."

"Help yourself, Shep. I know how you feel. Waiting always sets my nerves on edge."

A loud click as the door handle turned brought their heads up. Royce stepped into the room, followed by Jon.

"An amazing story!" Royce chuckled. "I don't believe I have heard it's like in this country. Back in The Highlands, it would have been similar to the old tales of murder and retribution, but now, they see things differently. Old times and old ways are sometimes more understandable, but here and primarily in Oregon, we are on the brink of something new. Statehood. We are the first to set the rules of law and order, for the ones who follow. We must be wary that the laws we set work but are not so rigid as to be untenable. Similar to the way your young government made laws that had room to wiggle, so to speak."

Clasping a handkerchief in one hand behind his back, Royce paced the room, in deep thought. His cane tapped the floor when he turned or stopped to consider some idea. He looked at Jon then Shepherd occasionally. All eyes followed his countenance and froze when he finally stopped.

Royce let silence accent his next words. "I'll represent you, young McKinzey. You must put yourself in my hands. We have to be very skillful. The tightrope we walk is very thin and fragile, but by Jehosaphat, I think I can pull this off."

Deep relief showed on everyone's face.

Royce continued, "We have a short time to prepare. Jonny. If you remember anything else, even the smallest piece of information will be valuable. Keep paper with you at all times, in case some memory pops into your head. One other bit of our familiar history you may not know... Both the McKinzeys and the Stuarts have been cursed from the ancient times to always fail." Royce sat down, picked up his glass, studying Jon through thoughtful eyes. "There have been many examples of failure through the years on both sides of the clans. The Stuarts lost the throne. The McKinzey clan lost power after the Jacobite war. We find ourselves pursued out of the old country into the new." He poured himself a taste of Scotch and sipped. "Never paid much attention to an old witch's curse anyway." Sitting back into his chair, he smiled pensively.

Lyle broke the silence in the room. "Good, Royce. Now that you are officially Jon's attorney, I need to fill you in on some of my investigations."

Royce and Lyle were soon head-to-head. This time, Royce listened to Lyle, jotting down notes in his journal.

Shepherd poured his brother a drink. "To your future, Jonny McKinzey."

"It will be our future, big brother." Jon tossed down his whisky. He tugged at his collar, still remembering the rope around his neck. He did not want to feel it ever again.

Neither of them smiled, aware of the razor-thin edge they trod. One slip and all would be lost. Could the portent of an ancient old woman's curse have any influence on them in the modern new world?

CHAPTER 27

Shepherd closed the door as Royce Stuart left to return to his office. "Ya know, Lyle, we could sure use some more help. We got any deputies close by we could call on if things go bad here?"

"All my deputies are out in the territory." He pushed open the slats in the blind and stared through them. He got the other two's attention and nodded across the street. "Well, would you look over there?"

Shepherd and Jon sprang to the window. Quinn and his lady friend, Faith Anne, were standing in front of Springer's General Store. Quinn nodded, stepped back, and tipped his hat to her. She entered the store without a backward glance. Quinn stood there a few minutes before he moved.

When he banged on the door, Shepherd let him in. "What happened to you?"

Quinn was in town clothes. He wore a soft-blue pair of trousers, a white shirt with a starched button collar, and a dark-blue frock coat. His face was bruised and dirty; his clothes were disarrayed and torn in a few places.

"I just got into a fight. You know, you try to do the right thing by a woman and where does it get you? Right into trouble. That's where. You wouldn't have a snort around here, would you? I could use a drink."

"Sure, Quinn. On the desk." Lyle handed him a coffee

cup. "Fresh out of glasses. Looks like I'm going to need some more of that scotch whisky I'm becoming so fond of. Help yourself."

"Wasn't that the little woman with the big shotgun I saw you with? Faith Anne was her name as I remember." Shep peered through the blinds across the street. "She's walking away with another fellow."

Quinn moved over and lifted the blind. "That was the trouble." He swallowed his drink and sat down.

Silence filled the room as Quinn fretted about loosening his collar, taking off his coat, fiddling with his fingers. He couldn't keep still.

"Give, Quinn. Give." Jon leaned forward. "What happened? Usually, the women are fawning around you like cats to butter. What happened?" Jon winked at Shepherd and sat down, trying to conceal the mirth bubbling under his skin.

"She…she…she said I reminded her of her ole dead daddy!" Quinn set his cup on the desk, eyeing the empty bottle of whisky. "To me…Quinn Taylor…reminded a beautiful woman of her old pappy. It's just not right."

"Why you got your clothes torn up and dirty?" Shepherd asked.

"I thought that man walking away with her was bothering her. I did the virtuous thing and intervened. All it got me was a punch in the face and a torn shirt. Faith Anne stopped it just as I was about to wipe the sidewalk with him. She said I reminded her of her daddy, interfering in her love life. For me to just go away…" He closed his eyes and cringed. "I need another drink."

After a moment, he opened his eyes to find the others trying not to laugh. "You all think this is funny! Hell, man, I'm Quinn Taylor. I'm known from here to St Louis city as the handsomest thing to ever look at a woman. Come all this way to have some little widowed woman in buckskins tell me I remind her of her old dead old pappy. It ain't right, I tell you. I'm Quinn Taylor, trailblazer, Indian fighter, raconteur, and gentleman. I got all dressed up and used my best perfume. All the way from Paris, France, it came, too. Smells real nice." Quinn sniffed his shirt. "All I got to show for it is a punch in the nose and a torn shirt."

"Raconteur?" Jon hid his face behind his hands. "When did you learn such elegant words? Mr. Trailblazer, scout, and Indian fighter! I know you're fanciful with the ladies, but where did you learn all of that?"

"I...I read it in books, damn you." Quinn held his head high.

"Books?" said Shepherd. "All of that is in books? Jonny, you didn't tell me you knew such fancy words."

"Not me, brother. I didn't learn that in any Indiana school."

"I read books. On the trail, I read a lot. That Dumas fellow from France. *The Three Musketeers* and *The Count of Monte Cristo* helped me with the ladies. Believe it or not, I used to be shy. I just acted like the dashing Count of Monte Cristo or D'artagnon of the Three Musketeers, and ladies loved it. I even threw in a few French words, like *mademoiselle* or *enchanté*, and I could take away any woman from any owl hoot with run-down boots from swamp water, Virginia. I must be getting old, because now, I'm as old as Faith Anne's old pappy."

Lyle fingered his mustache as he crossed the room to stand in front of Quinn. "I got a proposition for you. Somethin' to take your mind off all the women who have been turnin' you down." He smiled out the corner of his eye.

Quinn grabbed his head in both hands. "Not you, too, Marshal. My luck is wearing thin. Even my friends are making light of my consternation."

"I want you to be my deputy."

Quinn looked up. "What?"

"I'd like you to be a deputy. We're real shorthanded,

and with this trial coming up, I need a good man. An inside man. Someone I can trust. It'll be a hard job. You up for it?"

"What do you want me to do?"

Lyle went over to his cupboard and moved things around. "I want you to be my man on the street. Play some Faro, gamble a little. Buy fellas a few drinks. Keep your ears open to any trouble that may be brewing. Jonah Smith may have had some pals around that have the same grudge on Jon over there." He pulled out another bottle of Scotch. "This will soothe your heartache a little. Do we have an agreement?"

"I can do it, Marshal." Quinn found his cup on the table and held it up for a share of the whisky.

"Don't let anybody know you're working for me. It may cost you your life. We have to work out any angle we can find to get Jon out of this mess."

"How do I report any news or gossip I hear?" Quinn slowly sipped his whisky.

"Knock on the back door after midnight. Two, one, two will be our signal. Either knock or make some kinda sign using that pattern. Keep it brief and to the point. I'll front you fifty dollars to get you started."

"Do I keep any winnings?" Quinn's grinned.

"Let's just say, if you have anything left over after the trial and you can pay back the fifty, we'll split any winnings, fifty-fifty. Deal?"

"Deal, Marshal."

They shook hands.

Lyle counted out fifty dollars onto his desk. "Be mighty careful, son."

"I'm better with cards than with women, Marshal. I hope to give this all back to you and then some. Don't worry, I'll keep my head on a swivel and my ears open. Jonny is a friend of mine. I'll not let anything happen to him." Quinn put the money in his hat, took one more drink then left the office.

CHAPTER 28

———— ◆·◁◈▷·◆ ————

"I sure hope he'll be all right," Shepherd told Lyle after Quinn left. He watched through the lookout port in the door as his friend crossed the street to the saloon next to the mercantile store.

"Pshaw! Shep, you're talking about the best scout this side of the Green River. I've seen him walk through snakes, kill Indians with a tomahawk, and ride the hair off a stubborn blue roan stallion. I'm not too worried about another man up against Quinn Taylor. I just hope his broken heart don't kill him." Jon stole another drink when Lyle looked out the blind. "Quinn ain't used to thinkin' he's getting old and a lady preferrin' another fella over him. It may break his heart for good."

Lyle sat on his desk with his left hand balanced on his left knee. "My wish for Quinn Taylor is to get in one big-ass poker game and win some money then come over and tell me everything is all right about town, but it ain't going to happen, I'm afraid."

"Goin' on patrol, Marshal." Shepherd checked the loads of his shotgun, touched his pistol handle to be sure it was where he knew it to be. "I'll pass by here again in about half an hour, then I will finish about an hour or so later. Going to give a look in The Scarlet Lady saloon Quinn went into. If you hear shooting, comma running." He pulled the brim of his hat down to shield his face from the lowering late-afternoon sun then looked up and down the street, alert to any trouble.

The street was ankle-deep in mud and manure, Shepherd avoided holes and splashes from passing wagons, keeping the slop from his pants and clothes. After stomping off his boots, he read The Scarlet Lady in fanciful colors on the sign overhead that covered the large framed entrance as he began his patrol on the other side of the street.

Miners, sawmill workers, lumberjacks, traveling salesmen, and confused pilgrims wandered these streets. Shepherd stuck his head in from store to store to let shopkeepers know he was on the job.

Lyle had taught him just their presence alone was enough to tone down the riffraff and keep a semblance of law and order. The town was raw and fresh, innocently bursting with new industry and river traffic.

A woman across the street waved a handkerchief to him. He crossed against the flowing traffic.

"What can I help you with, ma'am?" Shepherd tried to see inside the store.

"Would you please tell that man to leave my store. He is trying to sell me a pig's ear for a silk purse. He thinks I'm stupid, but I am on to his ways. I can't get him to leave. I'm afraid he will try to rob me."

Shepherd opened the door with one arm, his other hand on the handle of his pistol. "Ms. Parsons says she has asked you to leave."

"I er, I was just going, Deputy."

The little man pulled his green derby down on his head snugly, picked up a carpet valise, and left the premises. "Thank you, ma'am," he said as he escaped out the door.

"You came just in time, Deputy. I don't know what I would have done with him."

"Happy to be of service, Ms. Parsons. Call on me

anytime."

After throwing the grifter out, he checked in with the local blacksmith. The assayer's office was busy. Gold was flowing out of the hills, boosting the local bars and saloons and, eventually, the local economy. Salem seemed to be industrious, but he knew the rank odor of villainy fermented under the surface.

I guess, I'll go check on Quinn. Nothing to be seen here. He waved and nodded to familiar faces he passed. His badge was his introduction to strangers. Some didn't like having a Negro deputy telling them what to do, but since he was a federal deputy, the exclusion laws didn't apply to him. Secretly, he enjoyed the consternation in some of their faces as he was greeted.

The doors of The Scarlet Lady opened, and a man stumbled out, red -aced and stinking of whiskey. Shepherd stepped out of the man's way.

He entered the cool, darkened saloon, and whiskey, human sour stink, cigar and pipe smoke, mixed with perfume from the scarlet girls enveloped him. The scarlet girls were the saloon's bar girls. Dressed in bright red, they moved among the city's elites and elite less, selling drinks and stolen kisses.

Shepherd motioned for the bartender. "Walter, is Quinn around?"

"Quinn is in the big game in the private room." Walter paused for a moment. "Drink?"

"Uh, sure, Walter, give me a ginger beer. I'll be right back." Shep headed to the back of the room.

Quiet descended on the conversation as he worked his way to a glass door at the rear of the main parlor. "Private" was etched into the milk-glassed window on the door.

"Shepherd, what are you doing here?" A surly man, with a huge bowie knife strapped across his chest, stepped forward.

"Dodgie, is Quinn in there? How's he doing?" He tried

looking through the glass where it was clear.

"He's doing pretty good from what I hear. Some green horn has been sulky 'cause he's losing his money. I'm letting the boss know you're here. We always let the law in. Keeps the peace when things get edgy."

Raised voices filtered through the door, and something crashed to the floor.

"I'm going in, Dodgie, tell Scarlet." Turning the handle and shouldering the door open, Shepherd stepped into the crowded lesser parlor of the The Scarlet Lady.

A circle of men had stepped away from around a poker table in anticipation of trouble.

A man in a dark-blue hat slammed his hand down on the table, making the chips jump. "I said you're a cheat, mister. I think you're trickin' me somehow," he screamed at Quinn. His hand went to his hip.

Quinn looked up sharply. "Hold your hand, Porter. I ain't no cheat. You're a damn bad poker player."

A sharp blast concussed through the room, cutting Porter's draw short.

"I watched the whole thing, Porter. This man doesn't cheat. You're just dirt poor at playing poker." Scarlet held a smoking coach gun in her hands. "This is my place. I won't abide cheating. Now put that gun back where you had it, sit down and play, or get out!"

"I'll get out, and I won't come back." The man picked up his chips and exited the room, pushing anyone close by out of his way.

Quinn caught sight of Shepherd, and he gave a faint nod.

"Nice crowd," Shepherd said to Scarlet.

"Glad to see you. Heard you were back in town." She returned to her seat on an elevated platform where she could see over the crowds and watch the action. Propping her shotgun up against her chair, she settled back and looked at him. "Is it true you brought your brother back for trial? I don't know him, but are you out of your mind?"

"Trying to clear Jonny's name, so he can live a normal life. We got a ranch. We both want families and kids. Livin' on the run ain't in our plans. Some feel, like me, his revenge was justified. Royce Stuart is his lawyer. We got to try it this way first."

"Royce is a good man. If anyone can get him off, he can. What brought you in today?"

"Just going about my rounds is all. Wanted to see how Quinn was doing. He's nursing a broken heart."

"His heart must be mending pretty fast. He's winning and wiping out everyone at his table. If that first gent hadn't called him, those two sitting across from him were on the verge. I've been watching your friend. He's very good or very clever. I can't see any chicanery from him, but either way, he might get himself shot."

"I'm finished boys. Thanks for playing." Quinn gathered his chips to cash out.

Two men sitting across from Quinn stood up.

One said, "You're not going to give us a chance to win our money back?"

"Calm down, boys." Quinn glanced at each man. "I'll be back this evening. You can play to get your money then." He raked his chips into his hat and left the table.

Quinn pushed Shepherd out of the way at the bar, as if he didn't know him, and ordered a beer. Under his breath, he whispered, "Me thinks something smells foul, as Mr. Shakespeare might say. They're coming tonight."

The clock in the office ticked louder than Shepherd had ever remembered. It ticked with the same beat as his heart. *Ticktock, lub dub, ticktock, lub dub, ticktock.* He walked around the office in his stocking feet so his steps couldn't be heard.

Two knocks, followed by one knock, and then two more

startled him. Gooseflesh flashed up his spine. He slid open the viewport on the back door. "Who's there?"

"Damn it, Shepherd, it's me. You know the signal. Let me in. No one is on the street."

Quinn slipped inside, crouched in a hunched walk. "I've kept to the shadows. I wasn't seen. Are you ready?"

"Yes, sir, I am ready. But I wish they'd get started. I've scared myself three times now. Lyle is ready. Jon is in position. When they comin'?" Shepherd sat on the desk. "Ya better take off your boots. We gotta be quiet."

"Soon, Shep. If the information I heard is true, they're coming at midnight."

"Well, it's seventeen minutes to twelve. We better get set."

"You think they'll come to the back door or the front?" Shep looked at Quinn with a which-way-do-I-go look on his face.

"These cowardly little men will try the back door, I'm sure." Quinn crept to the rear of the jail. "Tell Lyle, will you?"

When the clock struck twelve, Shepherd jumped. "Damn clock. Plumb forgot about you chiming the hour."

When a battering ram crashed into the front door, he turned. The front door burst apart. Seven men dressed in dark clothing entered through the splinters.

"We want McKinzey." They pulled up short, finding no one in the front office.

Lyle sat in a huge barrel on the back porch. "Hellfire! They started the fight at the front!" He rocked the barrel over. Crawling out, he grabbed an axe handle from inside the barrel then raced down the alley between buildings to the front.

Mounting the sidewalk, he yelled, "Wahoo. Here I

come, boys." He clubbed the closest man over the head then laid into another. He came from the back and surprised the invaders.

Shepherd and Quinn ran inside, armed with cudgels as well. It was too close to draw a gun with this many people in it, and each laid out the man closest to him.

Three men scrambled out the door into the streets. They turned, pulling their guns from their belts.

"Oh no, boys," Jon called from the jail's rooftop. He tossed a fifty-pound sack of flour down on their heads. Then another and another until they lay stunned, collapsed on the street, covered over in fine white dust. Coughing from flour-filled lungs, the men pushed to their knees, dazed and weak.

"Back door, huh, Quinn?" Shepherd poked his friend in the ribs.

"Okay, okay. It still worked, just like I said. No one got hurt or shot. We can have them available for the trial. The stupid bastards came into the jail. We didn't have to go after them." Quinn gave him his devil-may-care smile.

"It was a good call, Quinn. Let's get these boys behind bars." Lyle grabbed a man's arm to help him up. Clouds of flour floated in the air. "Come along. If you don't, I'll crack you over the head with my gun. Your choice." Lyle reached for his pistol.

The man shook his head and headed for the jail, trailed by a plume of white. His feet left white boot prints in the mud.

Lyle's men rounded up the bunch of would-be kidnappers.

"Who are they?" Shepherd nodded toward the two gamblers who'd spoken to Quinn that afternoon.

"Friends of the deceased from Gold City, and most were part of Trapper Jack's crowd, from what they say."

Shepherd opened the door to the back cells. "Gentlemen, divide yourselves between the back two cells. I will gladly crack your head with this axe handle if you so much as look cross-eyed at me. You got some answerin' to do on how Trapper Jack and Whitey burned our ranch and killed our pa. If not, you may be rotting in the territorial prison with snakes and Gila monsters.

Lyle stood at the door, looking at the street where citizens gathered. Some of the Chinese citizenry were busy scooping up the piled-up flour into round metal pans.

"What's happened, Marshal?"

"Ah, Mr. Trout. Our district attorney." He gave a wry smile. "Nardo, we just got our first witnesses for our side. Them boys will give you the real truth on what happened at the McKinzey ranch."

"I'll need to interview your boy as well tomorrow morning. Everyone all right?" Nardo Trout looked through the door where he could see the prisoners as they went into the rear cells.

"Never fired a shot, Nardo. Never would have believed it could be done, until Quinn convinced me."

"Good job, Marshal Newton." He turned to the crowd. "Thanks for showing up. Your presence says you are all concerned citizens. Our marshal thwarted a kidnapping attempt of one of the prisoners. I'm proud to say they did a fine job. Arrested seven men and never fired a shot. Seven with one blow, you might say. Just like the faery tale. All is well. Go back to your homes. Everything is under control." He waved to the crowd and went down the steps, keeping to the dry spots, tiptoeing his way home around the excited Chinese.

Lyle leaned against a post, crossed his arms over his chest, and watched the crowd disperse. He bit off a chaw, chewed for a while, and spit into the street. "This may get mighty interesting."

CHAPTER 29

Shepherd finished nailing the hinges on the new door to the jail with one last pound of his hammer. "There, that is done. That new door should hold out against any mob trying to get in here. It's four inches thick with iron window bars, iron locks and bolts."

"Good job, Shep. Seen Quinn around?" Lyle came from the back. He looked in the mirror, combed his hair then tucked in his shirt.

"He met up with some sympathetic ladies last night. We might not see him again until the morning of the trail."

"Would you tell Jon, that Royce, Nardo, and Judge Clark are coming to interview him again, this afternoon?"

"Sure thing. I haven't met Judge Clark, I don't think. What's he like?"

"Known Blade Clark since we were kids. Even fought Indians back at Bridger's fort. A few Shoshone feeling their oats, desirous of our horses. We escaped. Been friends ever since. Good man."

A thunderous clatter of horses clopped up to the hitching posts out front.

"Get down and be careful how you do it." A clear command came through the thick from outside. "Open up in there!"

"I've been expecting those boys. Shep, remember I tol' you we didn't have any deputies available? Well, these three were off on a secret mission. We'll see what they've caught."

A strong pounding came from outside, battering the door.

"Let 'em in. I hope you like the surprise." Lyle gave Shepherd a knowing look and waved his hand for him to see who beat at the door.

Shep opened the door.

"Keep those hands locked behind your necks. You've been enough trouble on this trip. Get up there, Manny. Why do I have to keep prodding you. You know where you're goin'."

A crowd of men pushed into the room, followed by three men with badges, holding guns. The first four had their hands behind their necks, looking cowed and exhausted.

"Welcome to Salem, pilgrims. I see you've come a far piece. Good job, men. Shepherd, meet some of your fellow deputies. On the left, that's Jebidiah, Jeb Logan. Next is Josiah, Joe Emmitt. Finally, the one in the sombrero hat, say hello to Bandy Taft. Looks like you did the job. Bet you could use a drink. Let's get them in the cells in the back first." Lyle opened the jailhouse door, gesturing for the men to move forward.

As the men moved forward, Manny shouldered past Joe, viciously elbowed him in the face, overpowered him, and took away his gun, forcing him to the floor.

"Stop. All of you drop your guns, or so help me, I will blow this man's head off!" He pulled Joe by his shirt to stand up.

"Damn it, Manny. You ain't getting out of here." Joe rubbed his nose. "You know that."

"We'll just see. Now drop them guns. You, too, black man. I know you and your little brother. I got nothin' against you, Joe, but I will plumb blow you to hell if they don't drop their guns." He looked directly at Marshal Newton. "I'll not swing for Whitey's killings if I can help it. Let us out of here, Marshal. Joe is a dead man if you don't."

Resignation filled Lyle's face. He had no choice in the face of a desperate man. He didn't want to report Joe's death to his wife, Annie, either. "You promise you'll leave and not harm my men? You do know we'll come after you?"

"I'll take my chances. At least, I know you're comin'. Joe and the rest just took us by surprise the other day. Take your hands down, boys, and grab their guns."

Lyle set his gun on the liquor cabinet next to his desk. "Better do what they say, Shepherd. Don't try anything. The rest of you deputies, do the same. I won't see you murdered."

"Tub, go let them other prisoners out of their cells. Bren, go round us up enough horses for everybody. Me and Smoke will guard them until we can put our marshal and his deputies in there."

The seven men from the other night filed into the room, smiling and greeting their friends, dispersing guns amongst themselves. Manny said, "Lock them up! My, my, my, I've always wanted to say that." He motioned for the prisoners to move toward the cells. "Make sure you lock them in there tight, Tub. We got to make some tracks out of this town, and I want some time to travel."

"Hey, look what I got here." Tub pushed Jon through the doorway.

"Well, if I ain't mistaken, that there's the man who killed Whitey Nolan and his brothers. We was coming for you, when those deputies surprised us. We found it a little suspicious that the prisoner is being guarded by his big black brother. So, we decided to mete out a little justice for ourselves and for the Nolans." Manny turned to go. "Wait a minute. You're just what we need. A hostage. It's almost too good to be true. Let's get mounted. Little Jonny McKinzey will lead the way. Anybody stops us and he's the one that gets shot in the back."

Bren came to the door. "Coast is clear, Manny. Not many on the street this time of day."

"Okay, take it easy, we're not in any hurry. Don't draw attention to our little party. We walk these horses out of town. Smoke, get McKinzey on a horse and tie his hands behind his back."

The cavalcade moved down the street with Jonny in the lead. They roused no suspicion or interest of any kind from the townsfolk, who went on with their business, like any other day.

Royce set his glass of lemonade down on a table. It was a pleasant afternoon on the veranda of his home. He, Nardo Trout, and Blade Clark were in deep conversation concerning the upcoming trial of Jonny McKinzey. Royce noticed the procession because Jon McKinzey was in the front of it. Instinctually, he knew something was wrong. He called the other men's attention to the group approaching the house.

"Be on guard, gentlemen. I believe veiled darkness comes out of the shrouded fen."

"What?" asked Nardo.

"He means trouble is coming down the street on horseback, don't you, Royce?" Blade Clark put out his cigar, as he studied the oncoming procession.

"I do indeed. Follow my lead, will you? But seek shelter. This may lead to a fight." He stepped into the street, checking the depth of mud with his cane as if he were just walking to the Oregon Spectator newspaper on the corner.

He looked up as the gang stopped, and waited for him to pass. "Oh, Jon. I was going to visit you at the jail today. Is everything all right? You look like you are in a bag of cats."

"You be careful what you say." Smoke laid his pistol across his saddle.

"Yes, Mr. Stuart. The tatties are out of the window. These Neds is boring me. They are galoots of the finest kind." Jon winked at Royce with relief.

Suspicion confirmed! "Would you come over to ma house for a wee blether, me wee yin?" Royce stepped closer to Smoke's horse, still looking at Jon. He saw the restraints on his hands, but still, did not look at the man beside Jon.

"I told you to be careful. What the hell are you talking about?" Smoke leaned closer to Jon.

"This one is a numpty ballbag." Jon inclined his head toward Smoke, a huge smug grin on his face in spite of his predicament.

"Aye. I see he is. I believe I'm about to do my dinger, lad."

"Dinnae tech your granny to suck eggs, my pa used to say."

"Hey you, Ned! Gie it, *laidy*." Royce swung his cane at Smoke's face.

Jon kicked his horse out of the way just as Royce's cane landed across Smoke's face, knocking him from his horse.

Shots from behind them knocked two of the escapees from their horses. Pandemonium broke out in the street. Errant shots missed Jonny as he used his knees to guide his horse back into the fight. Manny lined up to shoot Royce, but Jon ran his horse into him, knocking him from the saddle.

Shouts arose from behind them. "Seek cover! Get off the street. Go back inside!"

Quinn burst out of the hotel, slipping his suspenders

over his bare shoulders. He had on only boots and pale-blue pants and his revolver in his hand. "What's going on?" he shouted to the deputies.

"Jailbreak. They got McKinzey as hostage."

Men shouted warnings to people to get off the street and take shelter. As the deputies ran closer, the shouts changed to, "Drop 'em or I'll shoot. Get your hands up."

One rider tried to charge through the scrambling deputies, but Bandy leaped up and grabbed the man by his neck and pulled him into the street. The riderless horse ran, kicking his hind legs into the air until he disappeared down the street.

Lyle threw his hands up in the air at a charging horse. "Whoo, whoo!"

The horse reared, throwing the rider.

As the rider rose, he reached for his pistol. Quinn dove into the bearded man. They rolled in the street, cussing and slugging each other, until Quinn swung a lethal uppercut to the man's chin and he went down in a heap.

Nardo and Judge Clark shot into the fray, dropping men from their horses. Royce pulled the cover from his cane, revealing a deadly blade, and threatened to disembowel Manny if he so much as moved.

Marshal Newton ran to Royce. "You're all right, Stuart? Where's the judge and Nardo?"

"They are taking refuge behind the old juniper in my yard. Who is this scoundrel?" Royce pricked the man's shirt, just deep enough to draw blood.

"One of Whitey's men, trying to escape custody, using young Jon as hostage. The rest were part of the group of prisoners Bandy and my other deputies recently brought in, or one of the seven from the kidnapping attempt the other night. They escaped form the jail just a few minutes ago."

"You were locked in a cell, Marshal. How did you get out?" Jon asked.

"I can answer that, brother." Shepherd kicked a body

over to check to see if he was dead. "I made a copy of the cell key over at the blacksmith one day. Remember, I tol' you I'd get you out of town if need be. I kept it in a pants pocket, just in case I ever needed it. And I did." He smiled at Lyle, without getting a warm smile in return then walked to Jon's horse, pulling a large blade from behind his back. With a strong swipe, he cut Jon's hands free. "You are making a habit of getting tied up on a horse. Pa taught you better. Your arse is out the window."

"Give up on me, brother, or I'll skelp ya."

"Jonny, Jonny. You couldn't lick me in a month of Sundays." Shepherd laughed.

"Do ye aye?" Jon laughed in return.

"I didn't know you could speak in the Scot!" Royce said in astonishment.

"I said I didn't speak the brogue when I was a kid, but Shep and me used to go at each other all the time with the phrases Pa taught us. It brought back good memories, talking the brogue with you just now."

Lyle shouted to a muddy Quinn as he pushed his prisoner back to the jailhouse. "Hey, Quinn, please wear your badge next time so we will know who you are."

The other deputies guffawed at Quinn's plight, but they helped him, with congratulatory pats on the back.

Manny tapped Smoke on the shoulder then inclined his head to two horses tied just a few feet from them in front of the newspaper office. Smoke nodded. Quietly, they crawled away, listening to Jon and Shepherd as they talked to Royce and the marshal. Covering the noses of the horses to keep them quiet, they mounted, turned, and walked away from the group of men in the street.

"They're getting away," Jeb called, waving his gun at them.

Manny and Smoke broke into a run, firing back at men in the street, scattering dogs and pedestrians out of their way.

Jonny took off after them. Shepherd climbed aboard Manny's empty mount and galloped off. "Get 'em, Jonny."

All four men raced down the street. When Smoke's horse tried to leap over a pig lying in a muddy wallow in the street, he broke his leg, throwing Smoke to the ground. The horse rolled over onto its back, screaming in pain. Smoke pulled out his revolver as Shepherd pulled up.

"Drop it, Smoke." Shepherd held his gun to Smoke's back.

"I jus gots one more bullet, Shep." He shot the horse, and it stopped its thrashing, lying at peace. "I couldn't see an animal suffer like that." He dropped his gun and held his hands behind his neck in surrender.

Jonny raced out of town after Manny.

Manny rode without looking back. Desperately, he searched for a place to hide or to make a stand. He pulled up at the old mission church. After sliding off his horse, he ran to the doors only to find them locked. Using the butt of his gun, he broke the glass panes in the door. He looked back at Jon then disappeared inside.

This alarmed several men who were working about the grounds, and they stopped to call out to see what the trouble was.

Jon slid to a stop, raising dust and pebbles, concealing him from a shot through the mission window from Manny. Using his horse to shield himself, Jon went to the door. A rifle remained in the saddle boot. Jon pulled it out then checked to see it was loaded with a fresh cap. Bursting through the door, he dove to the floor and rolled over behind the back pew. Another shot splintered the pew just over his head.

"Got any left, Manny? That's either five or six shots, including the fight we just had. I bet you only had five shots. We all keep our hammers on an empty chamber to prevent blowups." Jon stood up, holding the rifle in his hands. "Come on out."

Manny slowly pulled himself erect, pointing his gun at Jon. "I'm a gambling man, just like Whitey." He pulled the trigger. The hammer fell on an empty chamber. "Damn." He threw the gun at Jon, hitting his arm.

Jon fell to his knees. His right arm had gone numb.

Manny raced away to the front of the church. He scrambled up a few steps then across the surface of the alter and into the choir seats. Trying the door to the vestment closet, he found it locked. Manny saw a connecting door to the next building and sprang for it.

One of the grounds men came through the door just as Mannie reached for it.

"What are you doing? I'll notify Reverend Lee about this. You're not supposed to be in here." He turned to leave.

Manny grabbed him by his shirt. The man fought back, punching Manny in the neck and dropping him to the floor, then he reached for the gun in his belt.

Manny kicked out, knocking the gun from the man's hand. Scrambling to get to the gun first, the two rolled on the floor. Manny coldcocked the man with the recovered pistol. Other grounds men came to the man's aid, jamming the door and blocking Manny's escape route.

"Get out of my way, McKinzey. I got no other choice. Hangin' ain't on my menu." Manny looked around . "There's no way out of here, 'cept through you." Desperation filled his eyes.

"Don't do it, Manny. I can take you in."

A feral moan rose up from deep within his being and then Manny rushed forward, firing wildly.

Jon shot him on the third step. Manny's body slid to a stop at his feet, the smoking gun empty and useless.

Shepherd pulled open the doors, looked around, and came in.

Jon went to see to the grounds man lying on the floor. "Ima all right. Did you get 'em?" He raised himself up on one arm, and the other men pulled him to his feet.

Jon nodded.

"Good, I'll report this to Reverand Lee after I go get checked at the hospital. I believe I'm somewhat woozy still. That was a wallop he gave me."

"Tell Reverend Lee it was the McKinzey brothers," Jon said. "He'll understand the troubles. We'll send someone for Manny's body when we get back to town."

When, Royce, Nardo, and Judge Clark came in unannounced, Lyle sat up at his desk. This didn't feel right to him. Jon's trial began tomorrow. It felt ominous that all three of the finest legal minds in the city were here at this time.

"Lyle, we want to see Jon McKinzey. Bring him out please." Blade Clark eased into a wooden chair, drumming his fingers on the arm.

"Shepherd, go get Jon, will you? Quinn, take a seat." Lyle composed himself behind his desk. He was nervous as could be. He didn't know what this meeting meant.

"Don't look so distraught, Shepherd, just a little something we have to clear up." Royce advanced to the liquor cabinet, found a bottle and glasses.

Nardo sat on the marshal's desk. "You're all going to want to hear what the judge has to say to Jon."

That seemed encouraging to Lyle, but he had his reservations when it came to matters of law. Evidence may be good, but some little misinterpretation could change everything. He didn't trust anything until it was finished.

"Here he is." Judge Clark sat up in his chair. "Jon, you have been charged with eleven murders. Maybe twelve, now that you killed Manny." He looked at Royce and Nardo. "The three of us have been to see the acting territorial governor on your behalf."

"Damn it, get on with it, Judge. You are driving me to distraction." Royce bolted back his drink.

"Yes, yes." Blade reached inside his jacket pocket and pulled out a legal looking paper. "We have negotiated..." Judge looked around at the other men.

"Go ahead, Blade. I want to hear it again." Nardo crossed his arms, intently watching Jon McKinzey's face.

"Er... We have negotiated a..." The judge let out a sigh and wiped his face.

"Jon, we got a pardon from the acting territorial governor! We convinced him that you had no other choice but to avenge the murder of your father and the burning of your ranch, since no other law enforcement agency in the territory did so. Your actions, in aiding and abetting the capture of another eleven men, who have been running lawless through the territory, was a large contributing factor. We also pointed out to the acting governor that it seemed likely his office would come under investigation if the truth of the elder John McKinzey's murder ever came to the attention of certain important Washington figures the three of us know." Royce saluted Nardo and Blade then took another drink. "The judge is holding your pardon and exoneration in his hand. You're a free man, Jon McKinzey!" Royce slammed the glass on the table.

"Thank you, Royce." The judge waved the paper. "This was his idea, and he was convincing enough to Nardo and myself to go see the governor." He accepted a glass from Royce, who was cheerfully passing out whisky to everyone. "His strategy worked."

"Is this really true?" Jon was in deep shock.

"Here it is. Read it for yourself." Judge Clark handed the decree to Jon, who took it with trembling hands.

All Jon could read before his disbelieving eyes was his name Jonathon McKinzey of Salem, Oregon...pardoned of all crime, dispute, or perpetuation, dated and signed by the acting governor.

"You did this, Mr. Stuart?" Jon looked out through damp eyes, still disbelieving what he held in his hand.

"Aye. We indeed did, wee yin. Along with some greasy gold that always seems to slip from one pocket to another among so-called political allies."

"Gold? We can never pay that back, Mr. Stuart. We appreciate what you have done, but the McKinzey's are not beggars." Shepherd took the drink from Jon and put his and Jon's on the table.

Quinn held his quietly down at his side.

"Hold on there, proud, Black McKinzey. Let's call it a debt repaid. The Stuarts owed a debt of gratitude to your clan for coming to our aid once long ago. It is now repaid." Royce took a drink and added more to Shepherd's glasses. "Besides, we have broken the old witch's curse that has bedeviled us all those years. Now, everyone, pick up your drinks. If ever a toast was to be drunk, it is now."

CHAPTER 30

Jon exited the jailhouse. "Marshal, I am grateful for what you have done for me and my family. We won't forget. Mr. Trout, Judge Clark, thank you for believing in me and Royce. I will call upon my return next year. Mr. Stuart, it has been a privilege and an honor. My family will be forever grateful."

"We are free of the witches, Jonny, and all debts are paid. Yours and the clans'." Royce shook Jon's hand while embracing his arm with the other hand. "I was just doing my job the way I saw to do it. Shepherd told me where you're going. Be careful. Second chances are hard to come by."

"Quinn, you have been as good a friend as could be. I am beholden to you. It will be the three of us building the ranch like Pa dreamed about."

"Uh… I been meaning to talk to you about that, Jon. I got a message about scouting for another big train forming up. It's what I do well. I think I'm going to take it. I feel cooped up in a town. I'm good for a few days. But then I get restless and itchy in my hands. I don't know what to do with them… But anyway, I'll come back after this next scouting job. I gotta settle down someplace. It might as well be here."

"You've always got a place with the McKinzeys." Jon smiled with understanding at his restless friend.

They shook a deep handshake. Shep came around with Derry and a pack horse and held the reins to Jon. Out of the corner of his eye, Jon noticed a raven sitting on a lamppost across the street, preening his feathers.

"I made promises, Shep. I'm going to the ranch and let Pa know I kept my promise, then I'm going to Eagle Claw's camp and marry Laughing Grass if she'll still have me. I'll be back within a year with a new bride. I know you will have things in order, and then we'll make the ranch. The ranch Pa dreamed of."

Jon mounted Derry, turning his nose out of town. He waved as he rode off.

A sharp croak and fluttering of wings startled Shepherd. The perched raven swooped down then glided away to position itself over Jon's head, leading him down the road.

Shepherd was dumbfounded. "Jon told me the story of the raven, but I never... I'll be damned!"

About the Author

Michael Lee released his first Western novel, *Del Rio*, June of 2022. He has created and authored a column on Native American Foods in *Saddlebag Dispatches* online magazine named "A Cowboy's Spoon," which is an investigation into the rich American Native food culture and history that developed 70 percent of the food the world now eats. He has contributed and published several articles and poems for *Saddlebag Dispatches* magazine as well.

He writes about the American West, wry poetry, short stories in several genres, theatre scripts, and makes bad attempts at writing songs from his poetry. He has won awards at the Ozark Creative Writer's Conference in Eureka Springs, Arkansas. A sustaining member of Western Writers of America, he is also a contributing editor to their *Roundup Magazine.*

Lee is also an active member of Critique Me Friday of Springfield, Missouri, past president of the Opelousas Little Theatre, and past board member of the Chiropractic Association of Louisiana. He is a gardener, forager, bowyer, home canner, philosopher, and *fantastic* cook. He lives in Southwest Missouri surrounded by the beautiful Ozarks.

Michael is available as a speaker for groups and book clubs, conferences and more. His books can be found on Amazon and other online retailers.